Sabine Baring-Gould

John Herring

A west-of-England romance

Sabine Baring-Gould

John Herring
A west-of-England romance

ISBN/EAN: 9783744780377

Printed in Europe, USA, Canada, Australia, Japan

Cover: Foto ©Andreas Hilbeck / pixelio.de

More available books at **www.hansebooks.com**

JOHN HERRING

A WEST OF ENGLAND ROMANCE

BY THE

AUTHOR OF 'MEHALAH'

IN THREE VOLUMES

VOL. I.

LONDON

SMITH, ELDER, & CO., 15 WATERLOO PLACE

1883

PREFACE.

———◦———

IN a tale of the West of England in which are introduced some of the lowest types of rustic humanity to be found there, it is impossible to avoid the use of the local dialect. This dialect has, however, been modified, as much as possible to render it intelligible without transforming it into the language of the schools. The vulgar dialect is regardless of gender and reckless in the use of cases. A cow is he, and a tom-cat wags her tail. At a trial in Exeter, at the Assizes, a man was charged with the murder of his wife, a woman with an aggravating tongue. The jury found a verdict of 'Not Guilty' against the clearest evidence, and, when the Judge expressed his surprise, 'Ah, your lordship,' said the foreman in explanation, 'us ain't a-going to hang he for the likes of she.' It is perhaps necessary to explain that 'the Cobbledicks' are no creation of the imagination—the clan has only been dispersed of recent years; the old man who lived in a cyder-cask is dead, but he was alive ten years ago. The clan was literally one of half-naked savages.

CONTENTS

OF

THE FIRST VOLUME.

JOHN HERRING.

CHAPTER I.

THE COBBLEDICKS.

'Log!' said the voice of Cobbledick the Old from a cyder cask.

'I be a logging like the blue blazes,' answered Cobbledick the younger.

Then a dry and dirty hand emerged from the cask, and with a gorse bush struck at the girl—that is, at Cobbledick the younger. She evaded the blow.

'Be quiet, vaither, or I won't log no more!'

'You won't?' with a horrible curse; 'then I'll make you, if I whacks and whacks till you be all over blood and prickles. There, I will, I swear. Glory rallaluley!'

On a spur of Dartmoor that struck out into the proximity of cultivated land, stood a

cromlech or dolmen—a rude monument of a
lost race, reared of granite slabs. This spur
of moor was a continuation or buttress of
Cosdon Beacon, which, next to Yestor, is the
highest point attained by Dartmoor, and is indeed the second highest mountain in the south
of England.

The dolmen was composed of four great
slabs of granite set on edge, two parallel to
the other two, with a fifth stone closing one
end. The whole five supported an enormous
quoit or block, plain on the nether surface,
but unshaped above. Local antiquaries, pre-
tending to knowledge, but actually ignorant,
called this erection a Druid altar, and pointed
to a sort of basin on the top formed by the
weather, with a channel from it to the edge,
and this they asserted was a receptacle for the
blood of human victims, and a means of lustra-
tion for those who stood below. Other antiquaries, knowing a great deal, and not ashamed
to confess ignorance where knowledge ended
and guesswork began, said simply that the
monument belonged to prehistoric times, and
that they neither knew who had built it, nor
for what purpose it was raised. The country
folk called it the ' Giant's Table.'

On the lee side of this cromlech was a
cyder cask, tethered to the cromlech by a

piece of cord passed through the bung-hole, and attached to a stout stick within the monument, entering between the interstices of the blocks.

In this cask lived an old man, named Grizzly Cobbledick by his neighbours. He had lived in the cask many years.

Some miles away, to the north, in another parish, that of Nymet, lived the parent stock from which he sprung, in an old tumble-down cottage, sans windows, sans doors, sans chimney, sans floors, sans everything save the 'cob'—that is, mud walls—and the ragged roof of thatch.

This hovel was what the Germans would call the 'Stamm-burg' of the Cobbledicks. That is to say, it was the ancestral cradle of the race; it was also the hive in which they continued to dwell. They lived there, apart from their fellows, with whom they held no communication, never entering a village nor dealing at any shop, never seen at market or merry-making, least of all at church.

Their unsociable habits went further. They allowed no one to invade their hovel and pry into their mode of living. If any of them saw a person stand still near the house to observe it, or to watch a Cobbledick at his work or his play, a yelp called the whole clan

together, and with howls and curses they set on
the inquisitive visitor, pelting him with stones,
and flinging sticks at his head, so that he was
glad to beat a retreat.

The Cobbledicks were half-naked savages.
They wore, for warmth not for decency, some
wretched rags. When the scanty supply of
garments failed entirely, then the whole crew
dispersed over the country, hunting by moon-
light for a fresh supply; they stole whatever
came in their way that could be converted
into covering to clothe their nakedness.
Anything served—a potato-sack or a flour-
bag. One or other would change into coat
or gown by making in it slits for head and
arms.

Once a farmer lost an oilcloth stack-cover-
ing. It was deliberately taken off his stack
one rainy night before he had thatched his
wheat. He recognised it torn up and utilised
as curtains to the open holes that served as
windows to Cobbledick Castle. The farmer
prosecuted, but first a rick and then a stack
was burned, and he was glad to stay proceedings and suffer the savages to keep his oilcloth, fearing for the thatch of his farmhouse,
and himself, his wife and babes beneath it.

When the neighbourhood was aware that
the Cobbledicks ran short of raiment, old

worn garments were purposely left out at night on hedges for their use.

The migration of Grizzly Cobbledick to the parish of South Tawton took place in this wise. It marked an epoch in the history of the race. The Cobbledicks had not arrived at that stage of civilisation in which property becomes personal. Their views as to property were undeveloped. The world belonged in part to the Cobbledicks, and the rest did not. What belonged to the Cobbledicks belonged to the family, not to any individual in the family. They owned land, reclaimed from the waste long ago, clay land overgrown with rushes, partly bog ; but this land was not the property of this Cobbledick or that, male or female, old or young, it belonged to all, on the principle of the Russian *mir*. Not only so, but the utensils of the house and of the farm were common, so also were the garments. The pipkin cooked for the whole family, and the hoe raised the potatoes for all to eat. The pipkin was not private property when Poll stirred it, the hoe was not private property when Dick worked with it, and the potato-sack was not owned by him or by her who wore it. If, by any chance, it were taken off, it thereby fell back into the common store.

The Cobbledicks never had been civilised.

They were autochthones. The oldest inhabitant of Nymet remembered them. They did not increase much, but they did not die out. Their congeners, named the Gubbins, lived in the Lydford glens in Charles the First's reign, when a poet thus described them :—

> And near hereto's the Gubbins' cave,
> A people that no knowledge have
>   Of law of God or men;
> Whom Cæsar never yet subdued,
> Who've lawless lived, of manners rude,
>   All savage in their den.

> By whom, if any pass that way,
> He dares not the least time to stay,
>   For presently they howl;
> Upon which signal they do muster
> Their naked forces in a cluster,
>   Led forth by Roger Rowle.

One night a star fell from heaven and descended into the hovel of the Cobbledicks through the hole in the roof which allowed the smoke of the communal fire to ascend; and this spark sank into the heart of Old Grizzly—he was not Old Grizzly then. What his name was then in the clan never transpired.

That divine spark conveyed to this particular Cobbledick the idea of personal property. This idea, once conceived, becomes to the social body what a backbone is to the physical organism. There is all the difference in social conditions between those who have accepted personal property and those who have not arrived at it, that exists between vertebrate animals and invertebrate polypi.

Cobbledick rose from his lair by the fire where he had been snoring, caught up a female for whom he had long been sighing, stuffed a wisp of hay into her mouth to prevent her from alarming the sleepers, threw her over his shoulder, and strode out of the Cobbledick hovel.

The dispersion at Babel was caused by the discovery of the possessive pronouns.

After having carried his burden beyond earshot, Cobbledick set her down, pulled the plug out of her mouth, and said, 'If you holler, I'll smash your head. So hold thee gab and come along of I.'

The female was overawed into submission, and she paddled along at his side.

When day broke they found themselves on a shoulder of down in close proximity to Cosdon. Rambling over the moor, the woman hopping and squealing as she touched the gorse with her bare legs, they lighted on the grey cromlech, and the male, curling his tongue in his mouth, produced a loud cluck.

The female, as an imitative animal, clucked responsive. ' Bags ! ' said Cobbledick male, and by this simple formula he had claimed the cromlech as personal property to himself, his heirs and assigns.

The idea of property had swelled to large dimensions in his heart since he had first admitted it. The tract of moor was at that time—we are speaking of seventy years ago— wholly uninclosed. Since that date many encroachments have been made, and much of the furzy waste placed under cultivation.

Xenophon opens his ' Anabasis' with the words, ' The Greeks began it.' In the record of the conquest and reclamation of the moor it stands written, ' The Cobbledicks began it.'

First they filled up the interstices between the blocks of granite of the dolmen with turf and moss, then they strewed the floor with bracken, and made bed and seat of heather. Then they marked out a portion of the moor, collected stones from off the surface with infinite labour, and fenced it round with these stones set as a dry wall. This they tilled, and, their appetite for property growing, they inclosed more. The tillage was rude, but then it was the beginning of tillage to the whole Cobbledick race. It took that race six thousand years to arrive at a crooked stick with Mrs. Grizzly dragging it, and Mr. Grizzly driving with a switch, and his weight resting on the tail of the simple plough. When he took his weight off, to quicken the motions of Mrs. Grizzly with the switch, the plough levered out of the ground, she fell, and he also was thrown forward on his nose. When Grizzly left the ancestral seat, he carried with him, in addition to a woman, two ferrets in a bag, and a sharp flintstone. With the ferrets he caught rabbits, and with the stone he flayed them. Grizzly was a neolithic man.

On their first taking possession of the cromlech, Grizzly fought his wife for the sack she wore. He wanted to utilise it as a screen for the entrance. The door was to the south, but the south wind is a rainy wind and must be shut out.

Mrs. Grizzly resisted, for the same heavenly spark that had brought to him the idea of appropriating one woman as wife, had carried to her also the idea of keeping as her own, her very own, the one potato-sack in which she walked and worked and slept.

This resistance on her part stimulated invention on his. He devised a screen of wattles and heather for the door, and this proved a better shelter than any sack could have made. Thus we see how the sense of property quickens

invention.   The heavenly spark never expired
in the breasts of the Cobbledicks; they felt no
desire, like the Apostles of old and reformers
of the present day, to revert to the conditions
from which they had escaped.   The spark
burned brighter, it demanded fuel.   They
proceeded to obtain a cow.   How they pro-
cured it nobody knew, though all suspected.
The Cobbledicks disappeared from Tawton
parish for several days.   When they reappeared
they were driving a cow before them down
the flanks of Cosdon.   Had they fished her
out of the swamps round Cranmere pool?
or had they gone far, far beyond, and acquired
her in the South Hams, and driven her across
the moor, leaving no traces in the spongy soil
and on the blooming heather whereby they
might be traced, in the event of those from
whom she had been acquired disputing their
right to make off with her?

But if this latter were the case, what labour
and perseverance it must have cost them to
convey a cow across brawling torrents, over
granite-strewn mountains, and through trea-
cherous bogs!

This was the way of the Cobbledicks.
When they wanted anything, they went
after it over the moor.   Beyond was El Do-
rado, between the pathless waste, a barrier

forbidding pursuit. They never robbed their neighbours of anything beyond turnips and field potatoes. They had made sufficient advance along the path of social culture to recognise a sort of fellowship with their neighbours, and to respect the property of near neighbours. But this sense of fellowship did not extend beyond the moor. On the other side was a sea full of fish, into which whoever would might dip his net.

One day the female Cobbledick became a mother, and Grizzly a father.

Soon after this the wife died. Grizzly dug a hole in the floor of the cromlech, just under where the fire burned, and laid her there.

She was pleased, when alive, to sit over the red ashes, spreading out her toes, and laughing at the yellow flames. Under the hearthstone she should lie, with her face to the ashes, and her toes turned to the blaze. The Cobbledick ideas were growing. The first dawn of that sentiment which in another generation might flower into poetry had appeared in Grizzly's mind.

But the experiment was not happy. At night, as Grizzly slept, he thought he saw the old woman working her way up out of the ground, throwing the earth forth like a mole, and then peering at him from a corner.

After that she dived again and disappeared. Presently he felt her heave the earth under him where he lay, and roll him over, so that he could not sleep. He was very angry, and he got a great piece of granite and beat the floor hard with it. But this was of no avail. Next night the old woman was heard scratching with her nails at the bases of the granite slabs. Once she had been given a hunch of saffron cake by a farmer's wife, and she had picked all the currants out and eaten them, before attacking the substance. She was now at work on the granite, picking out the hornblend, mistaking the black grains for currants. 'Her'll do with these great stones as her did with the cake,' said Grizzly; 'her got that all crumbled with hunting the currants, and her'll treat the stones same way, and bring the table down on our heads.'

After that he disappeared for three days, and when he returned he was rolling a cyder cask before him down Cosdon. This cask he brought alongside of the cromlech, and attached it to the old house in the manner described. He lined it with fern, and retired into it, along with the child, at night. He would no longer sleep in the stone mansion that was being undermined by the dead wife. He did not object to occupy it by day; and

when he ate, he always threw some crumbs or
bits of meat into the fire, to satisfy the crav-
ings of the old woman. He supposed that she
picked at the stones because she was hungry.

The child slept with him in the cyder-cask
till she grew too big, and made it uncom-
fortable for her father. One night he had
cramp in his leg, and kicked out, and kicked
her forth, head over heels ; then he bade her
go for the future to the old house, and sleep
there and be darned, glory rallaluley. Occasionally, in spring, when all is waxing and
wanton, the Methodists held revival meetings
on the down, and Old Grizzly was accustomed
then to prowl about the outskirts of the assembly, listening to the preachers, and to the hymns
and rhapsodical outcries of the converted.
These camp meetings reminded him in some
particulars of the ways of the primitive Cobbledicks. The new feature, unfamiliar to him, was
the association of religion with these orgies.

From such meetings Grizzly had picked
up a few cant expressions which he used for
rounding his sentences without in the least
understanding their import. If he began a
sentence with a curse, he finished it with a
hallelujah, much as a grocer, having put an
iron weight into one scale, heaps the other
with sugar till the balance is complete.

Cobbledick father and daughter were not in the unseemly condition of nudity affected by their relatives at Nymet. These latter so far resembled Adam and Eve in the period of man's innocency that they were naked and were not ashamed, but with the sense of personal property came the sense also of self-respect. The land on which Grizzly and his wife squatted belonged to the manor of West Wyke, of which the Battishills were lords, and the Squire took care that his tenants should not go unprovided with old clothes. The Battishills were very poor, and wore their garments till the last moment consonant with respectability; then they passed them on to the squatters, whom they made, if not respectable, at least decent.

'Log!' screamed the old man from the cask.

'I be a logging [1] like the blue blazes,' answered the girl, and she spoke the truth.

She was seated with her back to one of the great stones of the 'Giant's Table,' with a bare foot resting on the cask on each side of the restraining rope. She worked her feet alternately, so as to produce a vibratory motion in the barrel from left to right. The old man

---

[1] To '*log*' is to rock. Thus a logan stone is a rocking stone, and a woman logs her baby in its cradle.

liked being rocked to sleep; he exacted the task of his daughter: and only when he began to snore and ceased to swear, dare Joyce Cobbledick desist from logging and retire to her own lair.

The evening had fallen. The sun was set, but a haze of light hung like a warm hoar frost over the head of Cosdon, though darkness had settled down in the valleys, and the village of Zeal began to twinkle out of all its windows.

The air was still. The rush of the stream over the granite masses that choked its course was the only sound audible, save the fretting of the cask on the turf in its oscillations.

The girl was tired, and one of her feet was bleeding. She had cut it with a sharp stone that day.

Joyce Cobbledick was aged eighteen. She was a tall, well-built girl, with bright colour, a low forehead, and dark eyes. Her hair was as uncombed and uncared for as the mane of a moorland pony. It was dark brown. Her jaws were heavy and her cheek-bones high, like those of her ancestry. There was some beauty about her—the beauty of a fine animal; she was perfectly supple in every limb, admirably proportioned, easy and even graceful in her movements, unrestrained by shoes and cumbrous clothing. Her face was even fine,

but there was nothing like intelligence illumining her dark eyes.

She wore a thin print gown, and that
was in tatters from her knees by scrambling
through hedges to steal turnips, and brushing
through gorse brakes after rabbits.

Presently the girl intermitted her tramp-
ling movement, believing the old man to be
asleep.

The stars were coming out. The one street
of Zeal, lying between rich meadows and
wood, was like a necklace of diamonds em-
bedded in black velvet.

Joyce leaned forwards to listen if her
father were snoring. All was still in the
cask, preternaturally still.

She bent her head lower. Then, suddenly,
with a roar, 'Darn your eyes, glory rallaluley!' an old grey, frowzy head and face
shot out of the barrel, and with it a long arm.
A heavy blow of the furze bush fell across
the girl's head and cheek, making her cry out
with pain.

She recovered her position in a moment,
and dashed her feet together savagely at the
cask. The violence of the action was more
than the cord could endure, already fretted
against the rugged edges of the granite blocks.
It snapped, and in a moment the cask was

driven forward by the impetus of Joyce's angry kick. It rolled over and over, ran down a bank, then along an incline of smooth turf, dashed against a stone which somewhat diverted its course, bounded into the high road, where it shot forth its tenant, and continued its course in rapid revolutions down the road that here ascended from the valley. Joyce uttered a cry, sprang to her feet, and ran after the rolling barrel towards the highway, and there saw her father lying stretched across the road, stunned and speechless.

CHAPTER II.

WHAT THE CASK DID.

As Joyce stood on the bank about to leap down into the road to her father's assistance, she was arrested by a sight calculated to fill her with dismay. A chaise drawn by a pair of horses was approaching from the direction of Okehampton at a brisk pace. The cask was in full career down the road, gaining velocity as it rolled. A curve hid it from the postillion, and Joyce stood breathless, powerless to warn the post-boy or arrest the cask, watching for the result.

The boy was in spirits ; he cracked his whip, and stimulated the horses—fresh from the stable at Okehampton—to take the hill in style. The cask was whirling on. Then it reached the sweep in the road, and it went direct against the bank, danced light-heartedly up it, reeled back, swung itself round and shot straight down the road at the horses. In another moment it was on them, leaping at them like a tiger at the throat of his prey.

What followed was so sudden, and the light was so imperfect, that Joyce could not quite make out what she saw. She heard a loud cry from the post-boy, who was thrown. Whether one of the horses went down and floundered to his feet again she was not sure; she believed it was so. Next moment the chaise was off the road, the two frightened animals tearing away with it over the common. Forgetful of her father in the excitement of the spectacle and in dread of the final catastrophe, Joyce ran after the carriage, which she saw bounding over heaps of peat that had been cut and laid to dry, lurching into hollows, jolting over tufts of gorse, and jarring against stones.

Then she saw against the light of the horizon the figure of a man emerging from the window of the chaise, trying to open the door. Almost simultaneously the wheel of the carriage struck a huge block of granite, and in an instant the chaise was thrown on one side, the horses were kicking furiously, and the whole converted into a wreck of living beasts and struggling men and splintered fragments of carriage.

'Ho, heigh! stay them osses,' yelled the

post-boy, who had picked himself up and was
running over the down. ' Sit on their necks;
kip 'em down.'

Joyce ran also, and reached the spot soon
after him.

The postillion went straight at the horses,
regardless of everything else, and cut their
traces ; whereupon they ran off, and he ca-
reered in full pursuit after them.

' Leave the beasts alone, boy,' shouted a
young man who had disengaged himself from
the shattered carriage, and was helping out a
young lady. ' Leave the beasts and come
here.'

' No, no, sir! The osses fust. Them's
my concern.' And away went the boy.

' Here, girl,' said the same young man to
Joyce, as she came up; ' help me.' He signed
to her what to do, to raise a man who was
lying motionless among the fragments of the
carriage, to carry him a little distance, and
lay him on the turf at full length.

' Stay by him whilst I go for the young
lady.'

Joyce nodded.

The young lady was seated on the rock
that had upset the carriage.

' What frightened the horses?' she asked.

' I do not know. Are you hurt?'

'My foot is sprained.   I cannot walk; but
no bones are broken, of that I have satisfied
myself.   How goes my father?'

'He is seriously injured.'

'He did wrong to try and open the door.
The carriage must have fallen over on him.'

'Will you remain here whilst I go back to
him?'

'Certainly.   The moss is soft as a cushion
on this stone.'

'Your father, I fear, is seriously hurt.   As
you say, he was leaning out of the window
when the coach turned over, and it went down
on the side where he was.'

'Bring me my cloak from the chaise.   It
is chilly, and the spot is desolate.   Il me
donne les frissons.'   She spoke with wonderful composure.   She might have been on a
picnic, and the dish with the chicken pie
broken; yet she had narrowly escaped death
herself, and her father was lying dead a few
feet from her.   The young man looked at her
face, a little surprised at her perfect coolness.
The face was wax-like, of transparent white-
ness; there was no colour in it.   But then
she was cold and possibly frightened, though
betraying no fear in her manner.   Her features were regular and of extraordinary beauty.
Her eyes were large and the lashes long; her

hair abundant and black. Of emotion in her face there was none.

'I remember my father said he had suffered from the rheumatism. Pray take him from off the grass.' The young man thought to himself, 'He will never suffer from that more;' but he made no answer. He went back to the man lying on the turf, knelt over him, and examined him. Joyce stood by with arms folded.

'Is there any house near to which this gentleman could be removed?' he asked.

'West Wyke,' answered Joyce.

'Where is that?'

She made a motion with her chin, indicating the direction.

'And is there a gate to be had on which I can lay him?'

She jerked her chin again.

'Now, sir,' said the post-boy, coming up, 'I've got the osses quiet, what can I do for you?'

'This gentleman must be removed at once on a hurdle or gate. Run and bring me one.'

'Be he hurted cruel bad?' asked the boy.

'He is dead.'

'Deary me!' exclaimed the post-boy. 'What a mussy it weren't one of the osses. Make us truly thankful. I'll get you a gate.'

'I'll help you,' said Joyce. 'You don't look a sort to carry a gate. Do you call yourself a man or a rat?'

Presently the two returned with a hurdle; that is to say, Joyce was carrying one on her head, casting occasionally a contemptuous glance at the dapper little fellow at her side.

'Is my father able to speak yet?' asked the lady.

'No,' answered the young man. 'Do not be alarmed. We must carry him to a house, where he can be put to bed, and then we will return for you. Do you mind being left alone, or can you walk as far as to the house?'

'I have already told you that I cannot walk. You are forgetful, monsieur.'

'Then this girl will remain with you till we return.'

'Very well. If she likes to remain she may remain. It is her affair.'

The young lady spoke with a foreign—a French accent, which was pretty. Indeed, there was a foreign grace in her attitudes, and taste in her dress, which showed that, if an Englishwoman, she must have lived a great deal in France.

The gentleman returned to Joyce; he was a tall and fine young man, with dark hair and moustache and frank blue eyes.

'Will you remain here with the lady while we go on to the house?'

Joyce nodded and went over to the rock on which the young lady was seated. She planted herself before her.

'The 'ouse to which we must carry the gent be yonder,' said the post-boy. 'I seed him as I went for the gate.'

'Do not be alarmed if we carry your father.'

'I shall not be alarmed.'

Then the post-boy going before and the young gentleman following, they proceeded very gently to carry the motionless form in the direction of West Wyke.

Joyce remained with the young lady; she studied her with great attention from head to foot. The sky was clear, and there was still much light entangled in the upper atmosphere. The whole of the north was full of silvery twilight.

'I niver seed a born leddy afore so close,' said Joyce.

'I am a born lady,' replied the other, haughtily.

'Did I say you wasn't? Have you any other rags on but what I sees?'

'Rags!' indignantly. 'What do you mean, girl?'

' Look here,' said Joyce, ' I hasn't. Fust
comes the gown, and then comes I. Down in
the good land to Zeal and Tawton, where the
lanes be cut deep, I seed there be nethermost
hard rock, then over that comes shellat, then
a sort of gravelly trade (stuff), then a top o'
that meat airth; and over all, like the gown,
the waving green grass. Up here on the
moor t'ain't so. There's the granite and then
the moss, and if you scrats through the moss
you comes right on and on to the stone. That
be like us as lives up here, vaither and I, but
wi' the quality it be different, as lives in lew
(sheltered) places; they has more coverings
nor us, night and day, I reckon.'

' You have no more clothes on you than
that thin gown?'

' No, us be like moor rock, fust the moss,
then the stone.'

' Are you begging?'

' I never axes for naught ; what I wants I
takes.'

The lady shivered and drew back on her
seat. She was disgusted with the appearance,
and offended at the rudeness of the girl.

' Why don't clothes grow on our backs,
thick and warm as the wool on sheep, the fur on
rabbits, and the moss on moorstones? 'Twould
come handier,' observed Joyce Cobbledick.

The lady made no reply.

'Wot's that man, that young man as spoke to you and I?' asked Joyce.

'I do not know his name.'

'He don't belong to you?'

'Most certainly not,' with a contemptuous shrug.

'Where did you get mun?'

'He is travelling with us—that is all. He joined my father in taking a chaise from Launceston.'

'Why didn't y' travel by the mail-coach? Her goes by ivery day.'

'The coach had left Launceston when we arrived there from Falmouth, so we engaged a chaise. My father was in haste to reach Exeter, and that person joined us. I do not know his name, neither do I care. My father satisfied himself, I presume, of his respectability. That is all.'

'Where do'y come from, mistress? Over t'other side of the moor I reckon.'

'I come from France.'

Joyce was puzzled. Her geographical knowledge was too limited for her to know of France.

'I reckon that be a long way off, t'other side o' Prince's Town and the prisons, surely. Be there savages in them parts?'

' Savages ! certainly not.'

' There be here. I be one. I be a Cob-
bledick, and the Cobbledicks be all savages.
But vaither and I be better nor the rest out
Nymet. They be savages and no mistake.'

' I have no doubt of it.'

' I say, young lady, is that man as they
carried on the gate to West Wyke your
vaither ? '

' He is my father.'

' Did he bang you about much? Did he
whack you often wi' a bunch of vuzz? Not
but you'd mind over much wi' all them pack
o' clothes to your back.'

' Certainly not.'

' Did you have to rock him to sleep o'
nights in a barril? '

' No.'

' Mebbe you niver had much dodging out
of the way of the stones he throwed at your
head.'

' Of course not.'

' My old vaither doth all these to me.
He whacks me wi' brimmles and vuzz, and
he throws turves and stones at me, and I has
to rock mun every night or he wouldn't sleep
a wink. Of all the proper blaggards in the
world there ain't an ekal to vaither. But I
reckon vaithers is vaithers all the world over.

They be all like oaksticks, some crookeder
nor others, but none straight. You don't
mind over much what has happened to yours?'

The young lady only imperfectly understood the girl, owing to the rudeness of her
speech and her strong provincial brogue.

'There be my old vaither rolled out of
his barril right across the high road, and I
don't know if he've a broke his neck or no;
and I don't kear hover much, no more nor
you does because your vaither ha' gone and
done the same.'

'What do you mean, girl?'

'I mean what I sez. I know what broke
necks mean. I ha' broke the necks o' rabbits
scores and scores o' times. Him's just the
same, ivery bit and croome.'

The young lady shuddered. She did not
cry, but her breath caught in her throat.

'Mon Dieu! Ce n'est pas vrai! Comme
cette fille me fait peur!'

'What be that jabber about? You oughtn't
to mind.'

'For the love of God, girl, do not frighten
me. It is wicked—it is cruel. It is not
true.'

'Not true!' echoed Joyce; 'I knows it
be. I knows a broke neck in a man as in a
rabbit.'

'Be quiet. If you want money, *en voilà*, take and leave me tranquil.'

Joyce struck her hand aside.

'What'll you do wi' he now? Mother be poked under the hearthstone, where the fire can warm her. But when Old Grizzly goes, I shan't put he along o' mother. He can't sleep under the table now, and her'll lead'n a life of it, if he be put under the hearthstone along of she. Her niver worrits me, but her don't leave old vaither alone not one minnit of nights. Her does it because he knacked her, and beat her scores and scores o' times when her were alive. Now her thinks her turn be come. But her's got no vice in her. It be all play, only vaither be that crabbed he don't put up wi' it. When Old Grizzly goes, I'll up wi' his heels and send him into a bog once for all. He'll be wet and cold there I reckon, and the moss grows so thick over them quaking bogs, that once in there be no getting out, no more than when you're gone under the ice on Rayborough Pool. Then he'll leave me in peace I reckon.'

'You will do that, you long cripple (viper), you!' screamed the old man, who had overheard the arrangements planned for his interment, and disapproved of them. 'You will do that!' He rushed on Joyce from behind, raining furious blows on her with his fists. ‘You will stog me in a bog, will’y? I’ll put you in fust, curs’d everlasting rallaluley if I don’t.’ The old man yelled with fury. He stepped backwards and leaped at Joyce, and beat and swore.

The young lady was frightened, and cried out for help. The horrible old man seemed to her to be some superhuman apparition rising out of the moor soil—a vampyre, a ghoul from a cairn, come to destroy the wretched girl before her.

‘You chuck down thicky (that) stone, vaither?’ cried Joyce, as he stooped and took up a piece of granite in both hands.

‘I won’t, I won’t. I’ll mash you first, you unnat’ral varmint! You nigh upon killed me by rolling me over and over in the cask, and shan’t I nigh upon do the same by you? Glory rallaluley, blast me blue!’

Joyce was unquestionably stronger than old Cobbledick, and might have disarmed him, but the divine spark had been communicated to her; it flickered faintly in her dim soul, and a dumb instinct forbade her raising her hand against her father. She had borne his brutality for many a year, and had not resented it. She was his child, for him to deal with as he thought best. The sense of property had become strongly rooted in the minds of this branch of the Cobbledicks, and as forces are correlated, and heat, and light, and electricity, and sound are but the same force acting in different ways, so was it with the sense of possession. In the breast of Joyce it had transformed itself into a consciousness of filial duty.

Joyce put up her hand to ward off the . blow.

Then the young man who had carried the injured gentleman away arrived, running up, summoned by the cries, and with one stroke of the stick he held in his hand, he made the old man drop the stone.

'In another moment he would have beaten out your brains,' said he, panting.

'I reckon he would,' observed Joyce.

The old man howled with pain, dancing about holding his arm where struck.

'Who are you? What are you doing here?' asked the gentleman.

'Never you heed he,' said Joyce. 'Hers old vaither.'

'Help me away from this horrible place,' entreated the lady; 'I have fallen among savages in a dreadful wilderness. Am I in England, in Europe—or is this the wilds of Northern Canada?'

'She is lame,' said the young man to Joyce. 'Assist me in conveying her to the house yonder.'

Joyce put herself submissively on one side.

'How is my father?' asked the young lady.

'No better,' he replied.

'This strange girl tells me he has broken his neck.'

He was silent. He could not tell her the truth. It must be broken gently to her.

'I should wish to know if it be so.'

'Let us hope for the best. I have sent the post-boy to Okehampton for a doctor. He will know better than I what is the matter, and what must be done.'

'But you can surely tell me whether he be alive or dead.'

'He is still unconscious.'

'I know he be dead,' said Joyce roughly. 'What's a broke is a broke, and his neck be broke as sure as a bit o' cloam. I told her so.'

'Is he dead?' again asked the young lady.

She was now being carried to the house. There was no tremor in the arms that rested on the shoulders of her bearers.

'I asked you a simple question. It is unmannerly to refuse an answer.'

'I believe he is dead,' said he with an effort.

'I am very sorry,' was her calm reply.

The young man stopped; the girl Joyce stopped also. The twilight from the north-west was full on the white lovely face; there was no expression of distress on it, none of grief—not a trace of a tear in her large dark eyes.

'Why do you not go on? I said I am very sorry, naturally. He was my father. What else should I say?'

CHAPTER III.

WEST WYKE.

THE young man and Joyce conveyed the lady between them under a low embattled gateway into a small yard or garden—it was too dark to distinguish which—and halted in the porch of a house.

Joyce said: ' Stay, I go no vurder. I niver ha' been inside a house and under hellens (slates) afore, and I bain't a going now.'

The door opened, and a blaze of ruddy light fell on them. A young lady had opened to admit them.

''There be Miss Cicely Battishill,' said Joyce. 'Sure her will take my place once for all.'

' Another step more, girl,' said the young man to Joyce, ' and our burden is in a chair.'

' Why do'y call me a gurl?' asked Joyce. 'I bain't a gurl, I be a maiden. There be maidens in these parts and no gurls. I dunnow, but the leddy I been a helping may be a girl; hers different from I, I be a maiden.'

'Never mind distinctions,' said the young man, impatiently. 'Go on another step.'

'No, I'll put my head under no hellens. I be a savage,' said Joyce, obstinately. 'You go on yourself, and get Miss Cicely to help.'

'I will take your place, Joyce,' said the young lady at the door; and she assisted the strange pale girl to come in.

The young man looked back over his shoulder, and said, 'Thanks for your help as far as it went, maiden.'

Joyce stood without, the red light on her, with the dark garden, the moor, and the night sky behind, her strange face appearing even handsome in the glow, and the flicker reflected in her dull eyes.

The figure struck the young man with an evanescent sense of pity. She seemed an outcast—desolate, friendless.

Then the door closed, and the light was cut off. But Joyce did not leave. She stood in the porch with her arms folded looking over the black garden wall at the wild, blacker moor beyond, over which the wind was soughing. She was lost in a day-dream unintelligible to herself.

The light from the window streaked the

garden and fell on an orange lily that stood out luminous and fiery against the inky background of foliage and wall. The stars were coming out in the sky. Joyce remained motionless, with her eyes on the fiery flower.

In the meantime the pale young lady was conveyed to a seat by the fire. The porch door opened immediately into the hall or parlour. This was a small low room, irregularly built, with a bay in which was the window. It was so small that with twenty people within it would be crowded inconveniently; it was so low that a tall man could touch the ceiling.

The hall was panelled throughout, very unpretentiously, with plain black oak; there was no carving except over the great fireplace, where was a coat of arms, once heraldically emblazoned, but now obscured by smoke. The coat was curious. Azure, a cross crosslet in saltire, between four owls argent, beaked and legged or.

On the walls were hung a few old portraits in tarnished oval frames. The paint was cracked and peeling off.

The ceiling was crossed by moulded oak beams of great size, black with age and smoke.

A tall, very thin gentleman, Mr. Battishill, the owner of the house, and squire of West

Wyke and lord of the manor, had been seated
in a high-backed leather-covered chair beside
the fire. He started up and offered it to the
young lady with many rather uncouth bows.
This gentleman was old; he still wore his hair
tied back by a black riband, though the
fashion had gone out. His suit was rusty,
his boots were split in the upperleather, and
the elbows of his long coat were patched.
His face was peculiar. The nose was pointed
and aquiline, and, as forehead and chin re-
ceded, it gave his head the appearance of that
of a bird. The eyes were very wide open,
prominent, and of the palest grey. His hair
was frosted with age.

The expression of his eyes was one of
eager inquiry. His mouth was weak, and
the lips were incessantly quivering. There
was a kindly look about the feeble mouth
which assured those who studied the face that
a kind heart was lodged within, and showed
them that the qualities of this organ were
superior to those of the head.

Mr. Battishill's daughter Cicely was a fine
girl, about the same age as Joyce—eighteen.
She was somewhat stoutly built, with hair of
a glowing auburn, almost red, but not harshly
red, rather of the richest, sunniest chestnut.
Her complexion was of that quality, seen

nowhere but in Devon; transparent, delicate, white, with the brightest, healthiest, purest colour conceivable; a face in which the mounting of a blush had all the beauty and splendour of a sunrise. Her eyes were hazel, dancing with life and intelligence. There was buoyant good nature in every line of her face. At the present moment her expression was that of distressed sympathy with the lovely girl just introduced into her father's house.

The contrast between the two was striking. The new comer was absolutely colourless. Her hair was dark, almost if not wholly black. She was very slenderly built, her hands were long, and the fingers fine and tapering. The hands indicate culture and purity of race; those at which Cicely now looked were hands belonging to a lady of high nervous sensibility and perfect breeding. Her features were regular, and singularly delicately and beautifully cut. The eyes, when raised, sent a tremor to the heart of him on whom they rested; they were deep, full, and mysterious. A soul lay in those unfathomed pools, but of what sort none might guess. There was nothing in the expression of the face to assist in the inquiry. And yet the face was not a blank page and therefore uninviting.

The expression that sat on it was one of reserve, and therefore as provoking as those wonderful eyes.

Cicely was frank and impulsive; her heart was visible to all the world, she had no reserve whatever, what she thought she said; and her heart spoke through her eyes, a genial, affectionate heart, fresh and simple.

The pale young lady was evidently relieved by being placed in a chair by the fire. Her foot had pained her; it was now rested on a footstool.

' I beg your pardon,' said Mr. Battishill, ' I did not catch the name. It is such a pleasure to me to know to whom I am able to offer hospitality. It places persons on a footing of friendship at once when they are able to address each other by name.'

' My name is Mirelle,' said the young lady, without raising her eyes from the fire or moving a muscle of her face. ' My mother was the Countess Garcia. She married my father, a Mr. Strange. It is not necessary in Spain to take the paternal name; I prefer to be called Mirelle Garcia de Cantalejo. Cantalejo is territorial.'

Mr. Battishill listened with open mouth and staring eyes, and drew himself up. A distinguished guest this.

'And Canta——'

'Cantalejo,' interrupted Mirelle, 'is in Segovia—in Old Castile of course. We belong to the purest of the ancient Castilian nobility. Cantalejo belonged to the family from the earliest period ; it is even said that when Saint Jacques came to Spain he was the guest of my ancestor, and that is why we bear an escallop on our coat. Cantalejo belonged to us till the sixteenth century.'

'And now?'

'It has ceased to belong to us for three hundred years. But before that we exercised sovereign powers in the country, we coined our own money, and hung malefactors on our own gallows.'

'Your poor father,' began Mr. Battishill, his nervous mouth working and his eager eyes staring, 'that is, Mr. Strange—I think you said Strange—'

Mirelle bowed an affirmative.

'Your poor father, Mr. Strange, lies, I fear, in a very sad and precarious state. He has been placed in the spare bedroom upstairs, and the doctor has been sent for, but cannot well be here for an hour.'

'I am told that my father is dead,' said the young lady composedly. 'I am very sorry. And what increases my desolation is that he was a heretic.'

'You love him,' whispered Cicely, looking pained and puzzled.

'I have always prayed for him, and I will pray for him still,' said Mirelle. 'He did not know the truth, so his invincible ignorance may save him.'

'You would hardly like to see him now,' suggested Cicely.

'No, perhaps to-morrow.'

'You love him,' persisted Cicely.

'Of course,' answered Mirelle. 'It is my duty. But you must understand that I have not known him except by name till last fortnight. I had not seen him at all till a fortnight ago, when he came to Paris to take me away from the Sacré Cœur.'

The young man had been watching her face intently. He had seemed more pained than Cicely at her want of feeling. Now he drew a long breath, a sigh of relief; these words of Mirelle explained her coldness.

'I am sorry that he is dead,' she went on, 'but he ought not to have married my mother.'

'We cannot regret that,' said Mr. Battishill with awkward gallantry, 'since to that we are indebted for the pleasure of making your acquaintance.'

Mirelle considered for a moment, then she said simply, 'You mean that I should not have existed. True ; I did not think of this.'

Mr. Battishill and the young man were unable to repress a smile. She was a curious mixture of simplicity, reserve, and frankness. The reserve was exercised over her feelings, but she was perfectly frank about her thoughts.

'Have you ever been to Cantal——? I have not quite caught the name.'

'I have never been in Spain at all,' answered Mirelle.

'Where, then, have you lived?'

'In Paris. Where else should I live? One lives in Paris, one exists elsewhere.'

'But your father?'

'Mr. Strange was a Brazilian diamond merchant. I mean a merchant of diamonds living in Brazil. My mother married him there. It was very good of my mother, but she was an angel. He was rich—*comme ça, mais bourgeois.* When I was born, my mother came to Paris to have me properly educated, and I lived there till the good God took her. I have been at school with the English sisters of the Sacré Cœur. When my father came to Paris he took me away, to bring me to his home in England.'

'Where is his home?'

'He has none; he would make one. He
has retired from his business.'

'What relations has he? They should be
communicated with.'

'I do not know that he has any. My
mother never spoke of my father's relations.
She knew nothing of them; she did not
want to know them. In this world everything is on shelves, and the things on each
shelf are kept to themselves. Where they
get mixed there is inextricable confusion.
Above, angels; then kings, nobles, bourgeois,
peasants, monkeys, and so down to the lowest
form of life—those laid on the floor. My
father's relatives were not noble.' Then suddenly, 'Are you noble, sir?'

Mr. Battishill threw up his head proudly.
'My family is gentle, and of ancient degree,'
he said. 'We appeared in the Heralds' Visitation of 1620 in four descents, but I have
title-deeds that show we were lords of the
manor of West Wyke from the time of Edward
the Third.'

'Those are your arms?' asked Mirelle,
looking at the chimney-piece. 'What birds
are those?'

'Owls,' answered Mr. Battishill, proudly;
'owls argent, beaked and clawed or.'

Mirelle contemplated the owls, then looked

at the gentleman, with his blank eyes, beak-like nose, and grey hair. Her lips twitched slightly, but she was too well bred to smile.

'The bird is dedicated to Minerva. It is the symbol of wisdom,' she said.

'The Battishills were ever owls,' said he, proudly. Then he asked, glancing at the young man, 'Is this gentleman your brother?'

Mirelle looked up full for the first time into the young stranger's face.

'He is no relative of mine. I do not even know his name.'

'My name,' said he, stepping forward, 'is John Herring.' He was interrupted by a laugh from Mirelle.

'Herring!' she exclaimed, 'Quel drôle de nom! That is a fish they split and pickle, and pack in barrels, is it not?' The young man coloured.

'The name is bourgeois—Herring!'

The young gentleman drew back, wounded. He said nothing more about himself, but asked Mr. Battishill in a low voice for a lantern.

'The trunks and portmanteaus are lying with the broken chaise, and I must see to their being placed under shelter and in se-curity. Are there men about the premises who can assist me?'

'There will be some difficulty about finding a man,' answered Mr. Battishill. 'We
do not keep one in the house, and the cottages are at a distance. You will not find
your way to them by night. Do not trouble
about the trunks; leave them till morning.
No one will touch them.'

'I prefer removing them. When the post-
boy returns from Okehampton with the doctor,
I will secure his assistance.'

Cicely had lighted a lantern whilst her
father was speaking. She offered it to John
Herring. 'I will go for you to the cottages,'
she said; 'I will send some men to help you.'
She accompanied him to the door. 'It is
quite right that the things should not be left
out all night on the moor. There are tramps
on the Exeter road, and the Cobbledicks are
close by.' She opened the door, and the light
fell on Joyce.

'Why, Joyce, you here still? I thought
you had gone back to the Giant's Table.'

'If I were to go back to vaither, he'd kill
me. I ha' lost he his old barril, and him
won't sleep under the table a'cos mother be
there wi' her playful ways, tormenting of
he.'

'What do you mean, Joyce?'

'I means this, miss. His barril be rolled

away down hill, and I dunnow where her be rolled to. Where be vaither to sleep?'

'Under the Giant's Table.'

'That won't do, 'cos o' mother. Her be lively o' nights when vaither be there. 'Tain't wickedness, it be her playful ways. Her leaves me alone right enough. But vaither won't go there. Now if he might sleep i' one o' your linnies,[1] he'd be right vast enough as a nail in a door.'

'By all means let him sleep there, Joyce, at least for a while, till you can recover the cask.'

'Then I can go back to he. If I hadn't that to say, he'd ha' killed me. Now he'll go snuggle into the straw like a heckamall[2] in a rick. That's beautiful!'

'Joyce,' said Cicely, 'this gentleman is going to the broken carriage. Perhaps you can assist him to remove some of the trunks. They must not be left out where they are.'

'There be some scatt right abroad,'[3] answered Joyce; 'I seed mun, and the things be coming out like.'

'More the reason why they should be collected and brought under cover.'

---

[1] Lean-to sheds.
[2] A heckamall or heckanoddy is a tomtit.
[3] Broken to pieces.

'I'll go right on end,' said Joyce. 'And vaither may sleep in the linney?'

'Yes, he may.'

'Oh, rallaluley, he'll be glad!'

So Joyce led the way, followed by Herring, and Miss Cicely Battishill went in quest of assistance.

When Herring and Joyce reached the scene of the accident, they discovered Old Grizzly hopping about amidst the wreck, pulling the pieces of the broken carriage apart. He had made some clearance in the confusion, but not from disinterested motives. Everything in the shape of cushion and cloak had disappeared, and the old wrecker was engaged in collecting chips of the broken wood for firing.

John Herring did not notice particularly what he was about; it was too dark to distinguish much. He went directly to the boxes.

Of his own goods there was little to take care of save one valise, and that was safe. The rest of the trunks and portmanteaus belonged to Mr. Strange and his daughter. The trunks lay, some still corded, on the top of the chaise; others thrown off, one with its lock sprung. This box had either been very much shaken by the fall, or Grizzly's arm had been turning it over, for the lid would no longer close over the confused and over-flowing contents.

Grizzly Cobbledick decamped when he saw the lantern brought to bear on the wreck. Joyce called after him, but he made no reply. Then she went in pursuit to announce to him the glad news that he was to sleep in the straw of the calves' linney at West Wyke.

'I wonder,' mused John Herring, 'whether that old rascal can have stolen anything of value. If he has, there is no one to bring him to book. The owner is dead, and the daughter probably knows nothing of the contents of the boxes.'

If he had known!

CHAPTER IV.

MIRELLE.

IT is aggravating to the reader to be asked to move backwards when he has been well started in a story. He resents it, as he resents the backing of a train when he has left the station where he took his ticket, and is impatient to reach his destination.

The author is aware that he is trying the patience of the reader when he asks him to turn into a side alley which bends in the same direction as his starting point. He would avoid asking him to turn if it were possible to do so. But it is not always possible. To a drama, to the farce of half an hour, is prefixed the list of characters. In taking up one of Lacy's acting copies, the reader learns at a glance that Box is a journeyman printer, and Cox a journeyman hatter, and that Mrs. Bouncer is a lodging-house keeper. He learns a great deal about them before he comes to a word of dialogue. He is informed that Box wears ' small swallow-tailed black coat, short buff waistcoat, light drab trousers (short, turned up at the bottom), black stockings, white canvas boots with black tips, cotton neckloth, and shabby black hat ; ' further, that Cox is apparelled in ' brown Newmarket coat, long white waistcoat, black plaid trousers, boots, white hat, black stock ; ' that Mrs. Bouncer is costumed in ' coloured cotton gown, apron, cap, &c.' He feels at once that he knows all about these characters. He reads their past in their costume, they wear their souls on their limbs. Note that ' turned up at the bottom '—the words illumine the abysses of the character of Box, and make them clear to us.

But the novelist is debarred what is allowed the dramatist. He must haul up his curtain on a situation without an introductory word, and then, when the reader is puzzled as to the characters, antecedents, and purposes of the *dramatis personæ*, he is obliged to step forward, stick in hand, as in a waxwork, point out the several personages and describe them. This is the way of novelists. It is a bad way, it is inartistic, but it is exacted by the reader.

Now, in describing the characters of a novel it is not sufficient to give minute accounts of the costume—in the case of the Cobbledicks this is done in a word; the author is required to give his readers a key to the inner mechanism of his puppets, to show why they walk or pirouette, and what may be expected to be the limits of their powers. He can rarely do this without retrogression.

That Mirelle may be understood and not be judged with undue severity, we must step back to a period before her birth; but we shall be as rapid in our survey as we can, and shall resume the thread of our story after a very short divagation.

The Countess Garcia de Cantalejo was a poor Spanish lady sent out to Brazil by her relatives, who were by no means near, to be got rid of by marriage, malaria, or mosquitoes, as might be, but anyhow to be got rid of.

She was handsome, but, like the milkmaid in the ballad, 'her face was her fortune.' Now in Spain pretty women abound, and ugly women are exceptional. Marriageable men look out more for money, which is scarce, than for beauty, which is a drug. Money, moreover, they know, in prudent hands will wax; beauty they know, however well conserved, will wane.

In Brazil she was seen and admired by Mr. Strange, a diamond merchant, and she consented to give him her cold hand, intending at the earliest opportunity to supplement it with the cold shoulder. She married him because no one else would have her, and because he was well off. She was proud of her family, and it was a condescension on her part—like that of the sun which stoops to kiss the puddle—for her to link the proud name of Garcia with that of Strange, and Cantalejo—which was territorial, with a blank, for the Stranges had never owned any more ground than the six foot allotted them as graves, and that only till they had mouldered. They had made, but not coined, their money, certainly never had hung men on their own gallows.

Mr. Strange and the Countess Garcia de Cantalejo lived together for a few years like oil and water. At length the Countess became the mother of a daughter, who was baptized Mirelle at the font in the Cathedral of Bahia, by the Cardinal Archbishop himself. After this Donna Garcia informed her husband that their separation was inevitable. The child could not be decently suckled, weaned, and educated in a colony, certainly not in a city so mean as Bahia. The child, the heiress of the coronet and of the name with its territorial tail, must go to Europe.

The Countess did not purpose returning to

Spain; there were circumstances attending her departure from her native country which had embittered her against her relatives there. No! she would go to Paris, the centre of the civilised world.

Mr. Strange raised no objections. He was weary of association with a woman full of caprice, of fading charms, and of intolerable pride. He was a reserved and a disappointed man. To every bird comes its time of song; to the swan only at death, to the nightingale in balmy spring while mating; it is only the chatterers that chatter ever. The song time, the flowering time, the moment when the dullest life breaks into poetry, is the moment of love. Mr. Strange had gone through this and had been disenchanted, and thenceforth his life became dull, prosaic, without melody and colour, unimpassioned. His heart had flamed, and his wife had extinguished its fires with ice.

Mr. Strange had no love for babies. Babies are to men objects as offensive as naked infant rabbits. A doe eats her young rather than expose them to the strange eye before their fur is grown. If women were as wise as does they would never exhibit the contents of their nursery till the children could talk and run about.

Mr. Strange heard a squalling in the house; the object his wife had produced was thrust under his eyes and nose with indecent haste. It dribbled when teething, erupted with the thrush, and had a difficulty in keeping down its milk. Consequently, when the Countess proposed to remove the babe to Paris, Mr. Strange gave a cheerful consent, and this consent was made doubly cheerful by the certainty that the mother would accompany her child.

If Mr. Strange acted in a somewhat callous manner in granting this separation between himself and his wife and child, he was in other particulars generous. He made the Countess an allowance which, for his circumstances, was handsome, and as the child grew, and greater demands were made on his purse, he met these demands without remonstrance.

Arrived in Paris, the Countess Garcia had not long to swim before her feet touched ground. She had a perfectly legitimate right to her title, her pedigree was unassailable, her manners were polished. She appeared at the balls of the Spanish ambassador, and associated with the best French and Spanish families belonging to the old noblesse. It was well known that she had married a moneyed Englishman, of no birth, nor station, nor religion. It was known that she had married for money. No one spoke of Mr. Strange. The great people among whom she moved would as soon have inquired about a boil that troubled her as about the husband whom 'for her sins' she had saddled on her. No persons of breeding invite their friends to introduce them to the family skeleton.

Mirelle was brought up by the Countess to think of her father as a man who had taken a mean advantage of her mother's poverty. He was her father by sufferance; *de facto*, alas, not *de jure*. She had inherited her mother's complexion, eyes, and hair; the blood in her veins was her mother's, Spanish and aristocratic; her sentiments were her mother's, as also her prejudices and her faith. It was hard to say what she derived from her father except her living and schooling for which he paid. For that she owed him nothing. He was fulfilling his duty, and a privilege he ought to value. What was he, to be the husband of a Garcia and the father of a Garcia? He was English, he was a heretic, worst of all he was bourgeois.

The Countess bought herself silks with Mr. Strange's money, wore the diamonds he sent her, hired good rooms in an aristocratic quarter, and paid for them from his remittances. She had nothing whatever of her own. She owed him everything, to her handkerchiefs and her shoestrings. She knew this perfectly, and writhed under the knowledge. The greater the debt she owed him, the deeper the detestation with which she regarded him. Each present he sent her was repaid by instilling a drop of bitterness into the heart of his child towards him.

One stipulation with regard to his daughter's education Mr. Strange had made. He insisted that she should have an English nurse, and that when she grew older she should have English playmates and English governesses. When old enough to go to school her mother sent her to English nuns, because Mr. Strange refused to allow her to go to any other convent than one of English sisters. Thus it was that Mirelle grew up to speak English fluently and well, and to thoroughly understand the tongue. But of English ways of thinking and of feeling she had not the faintest conception. Proud, cold, selfish, and bigoted her mother had been, and the ambition of Mirelle was to model herself on her mother. Thus she, too, became proud, cold, selfish, and bigoted. It was not her fault—the fault lay in her training.

The Countess was a woman of the world,

who combined religious zeal with worldly self-seeking. She was a vain woman, and though she did her utmost to conserve her beauty it withered, and the child blooming into lovely maidenhood at her side made the contrast distressing, because noticeable. This was the reason why she placed Mirelle in a convent in her fourteenth year. She saw the girl often, but never, if she could help it, was seen in her company.

This separation from her mother was of advantage to Mirelle. It preserved her simplicity. There was no craft in her ; she was absolutely guileless, distressingly frank, and innocent of the trickery as well as of the wickedness of the social world. She was cold, because the spring had not yet come to her frozen heart. She loved her mother, but without passion, for her mother was too selfish to awaken passionate love. Her nurses and governesses had changed so often that she could not count them. Among the cold sisters, lilies of virtue, the exhibition of emotion was, if not sinful, yet smacking of imperfection. Natural affections were weaknesses of the moral spine, to be conquered by wearing a perpetual back-board.

Suddenly the Countess died—died in her chair before the looking-glass, reciting the

Litany of Loreto, whilst her face was being enamelled. The beautifier entreated Madame la Comtesse not to draw her mouth down on one side, it was cracking the enamel before it was dry—just when she had arrived at the ' tower of ivory.' Then Madame la Comtesse gave a gasp and the enamel came off, washed away from her brow by the sweat of death, and running in a milky river down her nose and cheeks, and dripping on the peignoir under her chin. The beautifier rang the bell, and said, ' Sacré mille diables ! To whom shall I send in the bill? Madame is no more in condition to pay.'

When Mr. Strange heard of his wife's death, he settled his affairs in Brazil. He was a strictly conscientious man, and he felt that now it was his duty to look after the child. He had no idea that the child had sprung up into maidenhood, and was a tall, lovely girl, lovelier than her mother had ever been. His wife had not taken the trouble to send him a miniature of his daughter. Miniatures are expensive, and the Countess wanted all the money she received for herself. She did, indeed, once send him a bit of her hair, tied with blue silk ; but then, that cost nothing. Mr. Strange thought of his child as a limp piece of mortality in a long white garment,

with a frill round the red head like that put
round a ham-bone—a thing of squeals, that in
its squealing showed a pair of toothless gums,
a quivering red tongue, and a crinkled white
palate. He could hardly believe his eyes
when introduced to his daughter. She received him with perfect self-possession, without raising her eyes from the ground to look
at him, for the sisters had taught her the
custody of the eyes. According to S. Paul,
there is but one Man of Sin, and he is in
the future ; to the religious all men are men
of sin, and in the present.

Mirelle curtsied gracefully. She spoke
the best copy-book sentiments of filial respect,
and assured him (out of the Catechism) of
the obligation to filial duty under which she
lay.

Then he took her away from the nuns of
the Sacred Heart, and carried her about Paris,
sight-seeing, in the hope of making her un-
bend.

The decorator sent in a bill for two
thousand francs, his charge for beautifying
madame, hoping to get fifty, and ready to
accept five. Mr. Strange tore the bill, and lit
his cigar with it.

An old woman who had laid madame out
asked five francs for her pains. Then timidly

produced a lock of hair she had cut off madame's head as she laid her in the coffin. The hair was beautiful still! and, oh! madame had looked so sweet, so peaceful, like a holy angel, actually young again. Then Mr. Strange took the lock reverently, turned his face away, and did not speak. Something in his throat troubled him. He thought of twenty years ago—of the time when his heart bounded, of the singing of the nightingale, of the flowering of the wheat, of the short dream of poetry. Then he recovered himself, and put something in the old woman's hand. The old woman went chuckling away. When she reached the street she said, ' That was a brave invention. Madame's complexion was that of a toad's belly. She was hideous as a monkey. I could not pick the paint off her skin. Some adhered, the rest flaked away. That lock of hair was part of her false front. Mon Dieu! how soft men's hearts are!' Mr. Strange speedily discovered that he and his daughter had about as many subjects in common as an Esquimaux has with a native of equatorial Africa. She was above all things a Catholic, he a Protestant. She was religious, and, because religious, somewhat conscientious. He conscientious, and, because conscientious, somewhat religious. His religion was to his life

what stockings are to a traveller's port-
manteau, something to fill corners with where
nothing else will go. With Mirelle religion
was the chief packing of her life, and this was
a condition incomprehensible to her father.
She had artistic instincts ; she loved pictures
and music. Now, pictures and music happen
to be two things not to be got in Brazil, except in such an execrable state of degradation as to be unendurable. But he liked the
theatre, and to attend the theatre Mirelle considered wicked. Mirelle had learned history
from the sisters of the Sacré Cœur—that is,
she had learned that every modern political
idea is positively evil, that absolutism is ideal
perfection, that the mediæval times were the
only times in which it was worth living, for
then the popes gave and withdrew crowns,
kings kissed their feet, and emperors held
their stirrups. She had been taught geography out of French manuals, and had learned
that France is to the rest of the European
powers as the sun to the planets ; from it
they derive their light, and about it they
rotate.

Mirelle had her acquaintances, the Princess
L'Amoureuse, Prince Punchkin, Countesses,
Baronesses by the score, the mothers and
aunts of her schoolfellows and friends of her

mother. Not one of these was known to Mr. Strange even by name, and when she spoke of them she might have been, for aught he cared, reciting the list of European lepidoptera.

Even in their eating their tastes were opposed. Mr. Strange was fond of pickles, Mirelle loved sweets. Chillies tickled his palate, chocolate soothed hers ; crystallised angelica carried her into heaven, and plunged him into purgatory, for he had a hollow tooth. Mr. Strange endeavoured to talk to Mirelle of her mother. Now that the Countess was dead some of the old romance that had surrounded his wooing reappeared, and his heart softened to the memory of the woman. Mirelle was ready enough to speak of her, but she had nothing to say that vibrated a chord in his heart. She spoke of her mother as a fashionable lady, living in society, dressing for balls, driving in the Bois de Boulogne, or holding a plate at the door of the Madeleine—not of her as a woman feeling, loving, suffering.

This condition of affairs was becoming intolerable. How was Mr. Strange to live with a young lady with whom he was utterly out of sympathy, whose head was where his feet stood, and her feet at his head ? They saw different worlds, they breathed different air.

The first thing to be done was to get her
away from France. That was a plain necessity. On English soil common interests might
spring up.

Mr. Strange had a friend of former times
living at Avranches, a friend of whom he had
lost sight for many years. He knew his address, and he knew also that he was married
to a French lady.

Mr. Strange's nearest relative, a cousin,
had lived formerly at Falmouth, and, he supposed, lived there still. Mr. Strange resolved
to visit his old friend at Avranches, and go
on in the packet from St. Malo to Falmouth.
He would consult both on what was to be
done with Mirelle. He had other reasons,
which will appear in the sequel.

So he hurried away from Paris, and went
to Avranches. His old friend was delighted
to see him, shook hands—both hands, with
the utmost cordiality, asked half a dozen times
after his wife and children, and forgot as fre-
quently when told that his wife was dead,
and that there was but one child, a daughter.
He insisted on carrying his dear friend
Strange with him to the café, and on his
drinking with him a glass of *eau sucrée*
flavoured with syrup of orange, and eating
with him sponge biscuits. Would he further,

in recollection of old times, favour him with a
game of dominoes? The Frenchified Englishman did not introduce Mr. Strange to his
wife, or ask him to bring Mirelle from the
hotel to his house, and finally, looking at his
watch, remembered he was due to take his
wife a drive, shook hands with his dear old
friend with effusion, and begged, if he were
again passing through Avranches on his way
to or from Brazil, not to omit to call and
drink again with him sugar and water and
eat a sponge cake.

Mr. Strange departed, his grave face looking graver. After a rough passage, in which
Mirelle suffered extremely, and her father
smoked and looked at the waves uncon-
cernedly, they arrived at Falmouth. Cato,
when at sea, jumped overboard, saying he
would rather die than endure another half-
hour of sickness. Cato was a stoic philosopher, Mirelle was neither a philosopher
nor a stoic. She was profoundly wretched,
and looked ghastly when she landed in a
drizzle at Falmouth. Thus her first arrival
in England was not encouraging. Mr. Strange
inquired for his cousin, and learned that he
was no longer at Falmouth; he had removed
to Launceston. Mr. Strange heard such an
unsatisfactory account of his cousin that he

was greatly disconcerted. His cousin's name was Trampleasure. He found a universal consensus of opinion at Falmouth that Mr. Trampleasure was a man unprincipled and unscrupulous, and that he had moved to Launceston only because he had made Falmouth too hot for him.

Mr. Strange remained a couple of nights at Falmouth, and then took coach to Launceston. There he neither called on his cousin nor stayed. He found at the inn a young gentleman equally anxious with himself to push on to Exeter, and he offered him a seat in the chaise he had hired. Thus it was that Mr. John Herring was with him and his daughter when the accident occurred. Before leaving Brazil Mr. Strange had made his will, bequeathing everything he possessed to his cousin, Mr. Sampson Trampleasure, and to his Avranches friend, in trust for his daughter, and had constituted them her guardians. This will was in his desk. He did not unpack his desk at Falmouth and cancel his will; there was time enough to do that on his arrival at Exeter. Man proposes: God disposes.

CHAPTER V.

THE OWLS' NEST.

WEST WYKE is a perfect specimen of a small
country gentleman's house of the sixteenth
century. Two or three hundred years ago
every parish in the West of England contained several gentle families, not acred up
to their lips, but with moderate possessions.
These small squires farmed a large part of
their own estates themselves, gave moderate
portions to their daughters, who were not
ashamed to marry yeomen and even trades-
men, and their younger sons went to sea,
or were apprenticed to merchants in the
towns.[1]

When the heralds came round to hold
their courts and examine into the claims of
gentility and right to bear arms, these squires

[1] Thus, in the Visitation of Devon of 1620, a Cholmondeley
enters his brothers as ' silkman on London Bridge,' and ' prentice
in London,' and a Wolston registers his sisters as married re-
spectively to a ' labourer ' and a ' clothier '; a daughter of
Glanville married a blacksmith of Tavistock.

rode to court with their title-deeds in their saddle-bags and their signet rings on their hands, and showed convincingly that they had held their acres for many generations and had borne coat armour. Hard drinking, gambling, an extravagant style of living, have destroyed these little gentry, and the same causes have effected the extermination of the yeomanry.

In the parish of South Tawton two hundred years ago there were seven families of gentle blood—the Weekes of North Wyke, the Burgoynes of Zeal, the Northmores of Will, the Oxenhams of Oxenham, the Battishills of West Wyke, the Mylfords, and the Fursdons. All have gone; their place is only known by the old houses they have left behind, and a few tombstones with their heraldic bearings on them in the church. The grand old mansion of the Weekes is now parted in twain, one half a farmhouse, the other a labourer's cottage. The park is cut down, the ceilings are falling, the panelling is decaying. The house of the Burgoynes is now a village tavern; Will, a cottage, its grand old gateway levelled with the dust; West Wyke is a farmhouse.

If we would know how our gentle an-

cestors lived, let us look closely at West Wyke
—it deserves a visit and a description.

The house stands on the moor, in the midst
of a little patch of reclaimed land. The situation is too lofty and exposed to allow of trees
to flourish. A few ash stems attempt to
live there, and they are twisted from the
south-west. A few feet below the surface
the roots reach the rock, and when the tap-
root touches stone the doom of the tree is
sealed.

West Wyke House was built in 1583—the
date is on it—by William Battishill. It is a
house which a substantial farmer nowadays
would scorn to inhabit. It consists, on the
basement, of one hall, a ladies' bower, a
kitchen, and a large dairy—that is all. And
that is the basement plan of many hundreds
of similar mansions in the West, once tenanted
by proud squires and their ladies, well born,
well bred, and well attired. Look at their
portraits—they were gentlemen of breed and
honour, they carry it in their faces; they
were ladies of pure and noble souls, refined
in mind, simple in life. It is written on their
brows.

In 1656 Roger Battishill, the reigning
lord of the manor, walled in a garden in front
of the house, and at the side built an em-

battled gateway, only twelve feet high to the crown of the battlements; a gateway of shaped granite blocks and carved granite mouldings; and over the centre, proudly also sculptured in granite, the arms of Battishill, the cross crosslet in saltire between four great owls. He planted the garden with lilies, white and orange, with honesty, golden-rod, and white rocket. These flourished here, sheltered from the winds by the inclosing walls; and a monthly rose ran up the side of the house, about the hall window, and bloomed up to New Year's day.

No road led to the embattled gateway. No carriages were used in those days, and for the horses' hoofs there was the spongy turf. When a rough track had been trampled through the moor grass, and made black with oozing peat water, the riders rode afield and made another way till the first had grassed itself over again.

Observe the date on the embattled gateway. Charles I. was executed in 1649, Cromwell had issued his edict in 1655 for exacting the tenth penny from the Cavaliers, in order, as he pretended, to make them pay the expenses to which their mutinous disposition exposed the nation. To raise this impost, which passed by the name of the decimation,

the Protector appointed major-generals, and
divided the kingdom into military jurisdictions
under them. These men had power to subject whom they would to decimation, and to
imprison any person who should be exposed
to their jealousy or suspicion. Now Roger
Battishill had been a Royalist, but his twin
brother Richard had been a Roundhead. There
were two other brothers, Robert and Ralph.
Now, when the commissioner came to Okehampton to levy decimation, he summoned
Squire Battishill before him ; whereupon the
four brothers, all habited in grey, with very
erect hair, protruding ears, and staring eyes,
and a general puzzle-headed expression in
their faces, appeared before him, and so bewildered the commissioner with their Roger
and Richard, and Robert and Ralph, and
their extraordinary likeness to each other,
and their profound puzzle-headedness, which
made it impossible for Roger to speak without
involving Richard and Robert and Ralph, and
so through the rest—that he dismissed them
undecimated, fully impressed that the Royalist
was Ralph, who, being only just of age, could
not have been in the past a dangerous recusant. Thereupon the four brothers rode
home to West Wyke, hooting with joy, and
in commemoration of this achievement set up

the embattled gateway, to shut themselves in
and the world and politics out for ever. Over
the gateway they carved the four owls, their
arms, said Roger and Richard, and Robert
and Ralph—their own portraits said the
malicious world of South Tawton.

Some account of the hall has been already
given. In our day the oak panelling has disappeared as fuel for the great hearth, but in the
granite mullioned window is still preserved in
stained glass the cognizance of the Battishills,
the four owls impaled with, azure, three towers
argent, on which are squatted three white
birds.

A gentleman of the present day, if not
exacting, might possibly accommodate himself in the lower part of the house, but
would hardly acquiesce in the upstairs arrangements, for there all the bedrooms were
en suite. In the centre slept the squire and
his lady, when he had one ; on the right
were rooms for the men ; in the furthest
slept the apprentices, in the nearest the
sons and brothers of the family. On the
left were three rooms all in communication.
The first was the state guest room, the next
that allotted to the young ladies ; beyond
that, over the cow-shed, the room for the
servant maids.

We have a great deal to learn from our ancestors, and we are learning much. We copy their architecture, we reproduce their dyes, we affect their costume, but we do not go back to their sleeping arrangements.

Some days passed. Mirelle remained at West Wyke; John Herring was lodged in the inn at Zeal, not far distant in the valley. He devoted himself to the affairs of Mirelle. Mr. Battishill was most kind, but quite unable to be of real use. He was prepared to discuss with Herring what must be done, and he would undertake to do what he thought desirable, but he never did anything. The dead man might have lain a month, three months, a year upstairs, before Mr. Battishill took steps for his interment. He had a theory of his own relative to the disposal of the dead. He believed that elm was an unsuitable wood for the making of coffins. Alder was the proper timber, because alder grew in swamps, and was presumably damp-resisting. It was in vain that Herring explained to him that alders did not attain a sufficient size to be sawn into planks. That was because alders were not suffered to grow; they were treated as weeds and cut down. 'Grow them,' said Mr. Battishill; 'give them time and see for yourself.' He would have allowed the dead

man to occupy the spare room till the alders
were grown.

Then, again, he had a theory that coffins
ought to be filled with that powerful anti-
septic, brown Norwegian pitch, pitch from the
pine, none of your villainous coal tar, but
brown pitch like old treacle. And so on,
from coffins to alders, and to Norway tar, and
the dead man waiting for the alders to grow
and the pitch to be extracted. John Herring
was obliged to see to everything, to arrange
with the undertaker, and to fix the funeral.
Then, again, Mirelle might have remained on
till she married or died for all that Mr. Battishill would have done to discover her relations ; perhaps it would have been better had
it been so. We take infinite pains to do what
is just and kind, and find afterwards that
everything would have been better had we
put our hands in our pockets. We give in
charity and pauperise ; we effect reforms
which bring in a state of affairs worse than
existed before. There is more mischief
wrought by doing good than by doing nothing.

Before the funeral, Herring discovered that
the deceased had an account with an Exeter
bank. He found this through a letter in the
pocket-book of the deceased addressed to
him in Paris from Exeter, acknowledging the

receipt of several thousand pounds, transferred by a Brazilian bank, and notifying the opening of an account in Mr. Strange's name.

Herring communicated with this bank, stated what had taken place, and the banker allowed him to draw a limited sum for funeral expenses. The young man requested, even insisted, on Mr. Battishill being present when he examined the dead man's pocket-book and purse, and he required him to sign a statement of the amount of money found on him.

Mirelle remained perfectly passive ; she took her residence with the Battishills as a matter of course. The accident had happened near their house, on their land ; it was only proper that they should shelter her. If she gave the matter a thought, this is the result of her cogitation, but actually it did not trouble her. She had always been provided for, and had never had to consider how she was to be provided for. She did not excuse herself for taking advantage of the hospitality of strangers, for it did not occur to her that such an excuse was necessary. Herring was obliged to take on himself what Mirelle omitted. He apologised for her. A strange chance had constituted him her guardian, at least for a while. She allowed him to arrange everything. If he asked her to advise him as to her wishes, she replied that she was without any ; he must act as he thought proper. She knew nothing of the ways of England ; he must do whatever was conventional.

It did not enter her head that his journey was interrupted on her account, and that he was put to very serious inconvenience by his difficulty in leaving her without a protector. To trust Mr. Battishill to do what was requisite was to trust a piece of bread and butter not to fall butter downwards.

Mirelle took it for granted that Herring was doing his duty or following his pleasure. She accepted his services as she accepted those of the girl who blacked her boots. Each fulfilled a function for which they were called into existence. She neither thanked him nor rewarded him with a look. What he was like she did not know, neither did she care. He wore very big and shapeless boots, but that was proper ; boots like these became a bumpkin.

At the funeral he wore black, and gave her his arm. He and she were the sole mourners. She did not wish to attend. She supposed that only men attended the funerals of males ; but when it was explained to her that this was not the custom in England, she submitted.

Mr. Battishill did not follow the coffin.

There was a difficulty with him about black clothes. He had one best suit, but that was dark blue with brass buttons. He was not provided with ready money, and a new suit of clothes would cripple him for some years, as it would have to be paid for in instalments, a leg and an arm at intervals of a quarter; the coat-tails at equal and similar intervals. Mr. Battishill did not like to admit this, so he was prostrated with a convenient attack of the gout the day before the funeral, and sat in his chair with the lame foot swaddled on a stool before him. We laugh at the shifts of the gentle poor, and label them meannesses, whereas they are necessities. Cicely remained at home. There was but one servant kept at West Wyke, a cook, housemaid, parlour maid, kitchen maid, laundress, condensed into one, and Cicely had sufficient to do to keep the house in order. A funeral, moreover, entails extra work—eating, drinking, and doleful making merry.

Herring gave her some money from Mr. Strange's purse, telling her that it was to be spent on things necessary, and would be accounted for to the executors. It was not right nor reasonable, it was not in the least necessary, that the Battishills should be put to expense by reason of the funeral of a man

who was an entire stranger. The deceased
was well off, and the small expenses of his
funeral would be nothing deducted from the
six thousand pounds which they knew was at
the bank, and would go to his daughter.

Cicely frankly accepted the money, and
made greater preparations than she could
otherwise have made. She put more saffron
and currants in the cakes, and with these
necessary condiments the luxury of candied
peel. Instead of providing cyder she put
sherry on the table, and gave the bearers and
undertaker cold round of beef instead of squab
pie.

As Herring and Mirelle left the churchyard after the funeral, she took her hand off
his arm, and in their walk back to West Wyke
she was interested in the ferns and mosses of
the banks. Herring spoke to her occasionally, trying to begin a conversation ; but she
answered shortly, and either dropped behind
to examine a fern or was arrested by the view
through a gate, plainly showing him that she
declined to converse.

When they were on the moor, John Herring suddenly stopped and picked a tuft of
white heath. He offered it to Mirelle, and
she accepted it indifferently.

'Although this be a day of sadness,

Countess, yet here is an omen that some brightness is in store for you. It is said in the West that the white heath brings good luck to the person that secures it.'

'You found it, monsieur, not I.'

'But I pass on my luck to you. Keep it; I hope it may always spring up in your path as it has this day.'

She made no reply, but gathered a sprig of pink heath.

On reaching the gate of West Wyke Cicely met them; she had been looking out for their return.

'Voyez!' said Mirelle, 'I have picked a lovely bouquet of ferns and moss and wild flowers on my way. We have no ferns in France, at least I have never seen such. In this one particular you surpass us.'

She showed her bunch. The white heath was not there.

'Oh!' exclaimed Herring, incautiously, 'the best flower of all has fallen—the white heath.'

'So it is,' said Mirelle. 'I am sorry; my hand was full.'

'Shall I go back for it?'

'No, it has fallen in the mire, and is trodden under foot. I shall doubtless find my own good luck some day myself.'

CHAPTER VI.

THAT OLD TRAMPLARA.

As they entered the garden, Mirelle was about to take Cicely's arm, and walk round it with her, looking at the flowers, when John Herring stayed her—

'Excuse me, Countess, I must trouble you one moment. I think it time that we should make an attempt to find out your father's relatives or connections in England.'

'I do not suppose that he had any.'

'Why not?'

'He did not speak to me of any. Besides, these people do not hang together like persons who have pedigrees.'

'But something must be done. Whither are you to go? What is to become of you?'

'Comme le bon Dieu veut!'

'You cannot remain here till some one turns up to claim you.'

'Why not?'

Mr. Herring was staggered. He could

not reply, and say that she was trespassing on the hospitality of entire strangers. She turned to continue her walk.

'That is a fine orange lily,' she said to Cicely.

'You must really allow me to detain you,' pursued Herring. 'All I ask now is, may Mr. Battishill and I look through your father's desk that is in his trunk? His bunch of keys has been given to you. Will you open the desk, or shall we do it with your sanction?'

'Do what you like, Mr. Fish.'

Cicely looked reprovingly at Mirelle, and ventured on a correction. 'Mr. Herring, you mean.'

Mirelle's cheek tinged faintly.

'I beg your pardon, sir. Your name had escaped me. I am not yet familiar with English names, which seem to me harsh or grotesque. I remembered that you belonged to the fishes, but to which particular family of fish I did not recall.'

Herring bit his lip, then said quietly, 'Would you prefer opening your father's desk yourself, Countess?'

'Mon Dieu, non!'

'Then will you give me the key, and allow us to examine the contents of the desk?'

'Certainly. But I do not know which is

the key. Here, take the bunch, and do as you will.' Then she turned impatiently round, and walked away.

When Herring had entered the house, Cicely said gently, ' I think, Mirelle, you are bound to try and remember poor Mr. Herring's name.'

' Why should I ? It in no way concerns me.'

' But you hurt his feelings. I saw he was pained.'

' Oh, but no ! that is not possible. He cannot care about such a droll name. Herring !—red herring—pickled herring !—the thing is ridiculous. When the name is historical, then—c'est bien autre chose. But when it is ignoble, and, in addition, is ridiculous, what is there to be proud of ? If there be no pride, there can be no wound. These people, moreover, have not the feelings that we have—I mean about their names. I should resent it were I called anything but what I am. But then the Garcias fought the Moors. Don Luis de Garcia with one blow cleft a Saracen through his turban, 'twixt his eyes, to the very saddle, and the saddle itself was cloven. We had the saddle and the sword in our armoury three hundred years ago. We held the county of Cantalejo, we

coined our own money, and hung on our own
gallows.   But the Herrings! they swim in
the vast sea along with the sprats and the
congers, the common plaice and the little
dabs.   They have no history.   They spawn
ten thousand at a time; they are the bread
of the nobler fish.   No—a Herring has no
cause to be offended if his name be forgotten.
There,' Mirelle laughed, 'I have said my
say.'

'He is a gentleman,' said Cicely, with
some warmth; 'I know nothing of his family,
but I judge by his manners and appearance.'

'I have noticed neither.   I do not consider those who in no way concern me.   I
cannot describe to you the colour of the eyes
and hair of the postillion who upset us, and I
know and care as little about the nobody who
had the bad fortune to be upset with us.   Il
m'ennuie, c'est tout dire.'

'He has been very considerate towards
you.   He has done a great deal for you de-
serving of gratitude.'

'For what else did the good God create
men but to be useful—to assist the ladies?
He made the dog the servant of man, and
man the dog of the woman.   The man does
not thank or consider the dog that fetches
him a stick out of the water, and the woman

has no occasion to pat and praise the man
who executes foolish trifles for her. If the
dog shakes himself near his master, when
emerging from the water, then the stick he
brought is applied to his sides, and when the
man makes himself over officious, woman
turns her back on him.'

'You have an odd idea of the reason why
men are placed in the world.'

'I have a perfectly just idea. At the
convent of the Sacré Cœur the good sisters
kept several tame men. There was old Jean
who sawed the firewood for them, and ancient
Jacques who gardened. There was even a
devout sweep who cleaned their chimneys,
and though his face was black, his soul was
white. There was a venerable chaplain who
heard confessions, and there was a domesti-
cated notary who did their legal business.
The sisters worried these men a great deal,
especially the notary and the confessor; the
latter made a good end in a lunatic asylum.
They all took it in good part. Their backs
were made to bear their burden.'

'You will not forget his name again ?'

'Whose name ? What! ce bon Poisson !
I will remember for your sake.'

John Herring brought down the dead
man's desk into the hall, that Mr. Battishill

and he might examine its contents together. Mr. Battishill hastily put his leg up as Herring entered.

' Sorry that I could not attend the funeral,' said the old gentleman, ' but the sins of the fathers are visited on their children. I endure the gout because my father and grandfather tippled port. Sit down, Herring, and I will tell you a good story. In the grand old days when there were many squires about here, and the Knapmans were at Wansdon, and the Whiddons at Whiddon, the old Squire Knapman was getting into a bad way financially, like me. He was invited to dinner at Whiddon, and drove there in his great coach. After dinner, Squire Whiddon saw him into his overcoat in the hall, and was about to accompany him to the door when old Knapman said, " No, no ! you will catch cold ; keep in, man." But the squire was too hospitable for that, and he attended Knapman to the coach. " Don't come out, for heaven's sake, you will get your death of cold," said Knapman. " Why ! " exclaimed Whiddon, " what is the meaning of this, Knapman ? Going to ride on the box instead of inside, a night like this ?" " I prefer it," answered Squire Knapman, proceeding to ascend to the box. But Whiddon would not allow it ; he went to the coach-door

and opened it—when, lo ! he found it full of
hay.'

' How came that ? ' asked Herring.

' Why, do you not see ? Old Knapman was
badly off for hay for his horse, and when he
went out anywhere to dinner he told his
coachman to fill the carriage with hay from
his host's rick, and himself went home on the
box.'

' A good story, sir ; but I think we had
better examine the contents of this desk before we tell any more.'

' Sit down, sit down, man. Do not drive
the willing horse, and let an old man give you
a piece of advice.   Let well alone, and do not
precipitate yourself, as Orlando says, " from
the smoke into the smother." '

' But you forget, sir, this that you advise
me to leave alone is not well at all.   The
young lady is an orphan, and we know nothing of her relatives.'

' Go on, then !   How full of briars is this
working-day world !   What do you propose
to do with the lady ? '

' I cannot tell till I have ascertained
whether she has relatives in England.'

' If she has not, she must be made a ward
in Chancery, or you must marry her, and so
take her affairs into your own hands.'

'Mr. Battishill!' John Herring flushed to his temples and looked down.

'I am putting an alternative case. Now, to make her a ward in Chancery is to put a fly into a cobweb. Her few thousand pounds will be bled away. By-the-by, talking of thousands, do you know any one inclined to speculate in silver lead? I have a rare lode on my property, but I have not the means to work it. I have set three men on the shode, and they have been engaged there for several days. There is no mistaking that grey-blue stuff that comes up. But I cannot go on myself. If I could, the property would be cleared in no time. As it is, I am crushed by that damned old Tramplara. Do you remember how Sinbad had to carry the Old Man of the Sea on his shoulders who picked all the apples and ate them himself, whilst Sinbad perished of hunger? Do what he would, Sinbad was powerless to dislodge the horrible creature astride on his back.'

'Yes, I remember.'

'Well, I am in the same predicament; I have got that old Tramplara on my back.'

'Who is Tramplara, sir?'

'Tramplara! Not know Tramplara? I thought every one knew and had felt him. He is a Cornish lawyer, who lived at Falmouth, till

Falmouth passed him on to Launceston, having had enough of him. He has lent me money. He knew that I wanted to improve my property; I was hot on draining at one time, and thought if I drained my marshes I should fill my purse. But, Herring, draining does not pay in all lands. It don't pay in clay at all. The only thing I drained effectually was my pocket. Then I was drawn on to speculate in Cornish mines that old Tramplara whispered great things of to me. As a particular favour he put me up to splendid investments before they were opened to the public. By all the saints in Cornwall—and they are more numerous than those in Paradise—that mining did for me completely.' The old man stamped his gouty foot on the ground. 'It was a swindle. And now I am entangled in the toils of old Tramplara, and cannot get out. Ah! Herring, if I could but work the lead mine myself, I should clear myself of Tramplara. But I cannot do it; the cursed rascal robs me of all my rents, and I am unable to nurse the mine until it can run on its own legs. I must call in strangers to form a company, and that means they are to swallow the cup and give me the dregs. Moreover, I am afraid of Tramplara finding it out. If he does; if he suspects what a lode there is at

Upaver, he will foreclose, take the property, and work the mine himself.'

'I have no capital at my disposal,' said Herring.

'I do not suppose you have. But only think! Supposing that Mr. Strange had come here alone, to recover of his fall, and that I could have induced him to sink some of his thousands here! Come along with me; I will take you to Upaver and you shall judge for yourself.' The old man jumped up, and walked across the hall to his hat.

'Your gout, sir!'

'Oh, that is all right now. A walk will do it good.'

'Another time, Mr. Battishill. Just at present we must examine the desk, and see if we can find any clue to the family of Mr. Strange.'

'To be sure, to be sure,' said Mr. Battishill, returning to his chair. 'You drew me off our business. Open the box and get the matter over.'

Herring was trying the keys. Before he had found the right key, Mr. Battishill put his hand on the bunch and said, 'By the way, before we go on with our inquiry, tell me, do you belong to the Herrings of Codrington?'

'I did not know there were Herrings there.'

'No ; I do not mean now. In 1620 Hugh Manning, of Newton Bushell, married Elizabeth, daughter of John Herring, of Codrington, in Devon ; so it stands in the Visitation, under the Manning pedigree. I do not think much of your family not appearing in that Visitation, as some good Devon families just emerging from the yeoman class, or not caring to appear at the court of the heralds, are left unregistered. It was so in this parish. Neither the Oxenhams nor the Northmores appeared, and yet they held lands here from time immemorial.'

'Had we not better seek out the Strange family, instead of exploring the past of the Herrings? The latter will keep.'

'You are right, quite right, my young friend. Good Lord, what pertinacity you have. It is like that of a ferret hanging on to a rat. Open the desk.'

The desk contained a considerable number of papers, almost all connected with business, and in a foreign language—Portuguese —which Herring could not read.

Mr. Battishill leaned back in his chair and looked before him out of the hall window, lost in his meditations. He muttered something impatiently.

' I beg your pardon,' said Herring, looking up. ' Did you address me?'

' I?—no,' answered Mr. Battishill. ' I merely said, Damn old Tramplara!'

Herring resumed his examination.

' The scoundrel has his claws in my neck, and the mischief is he is dragging more than myself down. There is poor Cicely as well.'

' Can you decipher these letters?' asked Herring, holding out a couple of papers to the old gentleman; ' they are written either in Spanish, Italian, or Portuguese.'

' I cannot say. My knowledge is limited. " Ignorance is the curse of God, knowledge the wing whereby we fly to heaven." I once read Latin, but that was long ago. I may remember a few words of French. " Dieu et mon droit," that means " God and my right." " Honi soit qui mal y pense," that means something about the Duchess of Gloucester's garter. No, this is Chinese to me. " There is no darkness but ignorance." '

' Hold!' exclaimed Herring; ' here is his will. Shall we look at it?'

' By all means. No other document is so likely to help you to what you want to discover. Give it to me.'

The will was very short. Mr. Strange had drawn it up himself before sailing for Europe.

The substance has been already given. Mr. Strange left everything he possessed to Mr. Eustace Smith, of Avranches, gentleman, and Mr. Sampson Trampleasure, of Falmouth, solicitor, in trust for his daughter, Mirelle, till she attained the age of twenty-three, and empowering them to expend from it such moneys as were needed for her entertainment and education. They were constituted sole guardians, trustees, and executors.

Mr. Battishill uttered a groan.

' That scoundrel again ! '

' But, sir, this is Trampleasure, not Tramplara.'

' It is the same. He writes himself Trampleasure, but nobody dreams of calling him anything but Tramplara.'

' He is constituted her guardian.'

' Yes ; but associated, fortunately, with another, Mr. Eustace Smith.'

' But should he renounce ? '

' Then good-bye to Mirelle's six thousand pounds. It will go down Wheal Polpluggan.'

' Wheal what ? '

' Wheal Polpluggan, that engulfed my money, and me.'

CHAPTER VII.

THAT YOUNG TRAMPLARA.

'WHAT is to be done?' asked Herring. There was a small black square ruler on the table, belonging to Mr. Strange's desk. He took it up and played with it, now balancing it across his finger, then standing it up on the table, with the end in his palm.

'Let things take their course,' answered Mr. Battishill. 'I advise with Gloucester, "Thy greatest help is quiet."'

'I will write to Mr. Eustace Smith at once.'

'Do so. If he renounces, mark my words, Polpluggan swallows the young lady's fortune. Friend Herring, I have the eyes of my heraldic cognizance, and can see in the dark. A wonderful mine, Polpluggan. The amount of capital sunk in it must have constituted a silver lode somewhere.'

'When I have heard from Mr. Eustace Smith I will communicate with Mr. Trampleasure—not before. I suppose I am justified in doing this?'

'Justified! Certainly. I have never seen Polpluggan myself. It is situated in the Scilly Isles. Of these there be forty; but I have been unable myself to make out in which Polpluggan lies, whether in Presher, or Bryher, or Annette, or Tean, or Great Gannilly, or Little Gannilly, or Gweal, or Withial, or Ganniornich, or——'

'I beg your pardon. May I borrow some notepaper?'

'By all means. There is some. The beauty, or the mischief of the matter is, that the lode of tin is in the granite and under the sea. Mining in granite is costly, and the proximity to the sea dangerous, entailing extraordinary precautions. The water gets in. Now when this takes place there follows a call on the shareholders for pumping it out. Every great storm drowns the mine and fills the shareholders with despair; the pump goes down into their pockets. Then the tin vein does not yield as at first. Once there were bunches like those of Eshcol, the dividends were seven, seven-and-a-half, eight, eight-and-a-quarter, going, going, going up, and then, slow but sure, as the miners sank their shaft so did the shares sink, and the dividends with them, till they reached zero. After that, a rapidly swelling minus quantity.'

'I have written the letter. Have you sealing-wax?'

'There it is. Now the beauty, or the mischief is—beauty from the Tramplara, mischief from the Battishill point of view—that old rascal so fired my imagination, and was so accommodating, that I borrowed the money of him to sink in Polpluggan. If I had speculated with my own little savings—but no! I had no savings—that would have been bad enough, but to speculate on borrowed capital is ruinous. That rascally old Tramplara led me on till he led me into his trap, and then snap, the door shut behind me, and I am fast. Poor West Wyke! Poor Cicely! Poor—' he looked at the stained coat in the window, ' poor ancestral owls ! '

A shadow fell across the table from some one passing the window.

'Good God!' exclaimed Mr. Battishill ; ' here comes that young Tramplara.'

A rap with the handle of a riding-whip on the hall door, and, without waiting for a response, Tramplara entered. He was a young man, good looking, with dark hair and eyes, and a dark moustache. His cheeks were florid. He had been drinking, and that gave a gloss to his face and an uncertainty to his eye. He came in with his hat on. He wore a short coat, knee breeches, and tall boots.

'I say,' he began roughly, 'what is the meaning of this? There have been those— with an oath—Cobbledicks inclosing a fresh piece of the down. I won't have it. They will establish rights, and it will be hard to displace them. Their fences must be tore down.' His pronunciation was West country, his grammar occasionally so.

'Have you observed that Mr. Battishill is in the room?' asked Herring, quietly. He had just sealed the Avranches letter.

'I see him right enough. I was addressing him, not you.'

Herring looked at the old gentleman; he had become limp. His jaw had fallen, and his hands trembled as he laid them on the arms of his chair.

'Then perhaps you will remove your hat, Mr. Tramplara.'

'I object to be so called,' answered the young man sharply. 'My name, sir, is Trampleasure, and only those who can't spell call me otherwise.'

'Very well, Mr. Trampleasure; will you remove your hat?'

'Who are you? I don't know you. Never

had the pleasure of seeing your face that I am aware of. What may your d—d name be, hey?'

'Sir,' said Herring, rising, 'I will stand no insolence. When you ask my name properly, you shall have it.'

'O Lord! who cares a brass button what you be called? Keep your name to yourself if you like.'

Herring walked straight up to him, composedly and firmly, looked him full in the eyes, and said, 'You have been drinking. Remove your hat, or I will knock it off.'

Tramplara took off his beaver and put it testily on the table.

'I am not a bad fellow,' he said, 'when asked a civil question, but I object to be bullied.'

Then he seated himself near the table, looking sulky.

'I am Mr. Sampson Trampleasure, junior, gentleman,' he said. 'Now perhaps you will tell me your name.'

Herring gave him in return his sur and Christian names.

'Never heard of you,' said Tramplara. 'What are you doing here?'

Herring made no reply to his impertinence.

'I say,' began the young man again, in a

loud tone, 'I won't have those Cobbledicks encroaching. I saw that old Bufflehead, Grizzly, but could not make him understand, or leastways he wouldn't understand.'

Mr. Battishill bridled up feebly. 'You are premature, Mr. Sampson; West Wyke is my property, and I have the right to settle on it whom I choose.'

'Oh, ah! that's good,' said young Tramplara. 'Yours on sufferance. You know well enough that my governor has his foot under your chair, and can kick you over any day he has a mind to.'

'When he does that he can deal with the Cobbledicks as well. Naked came we into the world, and naked we shall go out, Battishills and Cobbledicks together.'

'That'll soon take place unless you shell out. You know what I have come about.'

Mr. Battishill's brief indignation and assumption of dignity expired. He put his hand into his pocket, and drew forth his handkerchief, and wiped his lips.

'You have come on an unfortunate day, Mr. Sampson. We have had a death in the house.'

'I don't care whether there be a death or a birth,' answered the young man rudely. 'I know one thing, if I do not go back with the interest due last Lady in my pocket, there'll be pretty summary dealings in a place and with persons not the other side of London, nor in China, nor New Zealand, nor Bra——! Why! how in the name of Ginger came this into your hands?'

His eye was resting on the will that lay open as John Herring had left it when extracting from it the address of Mr. Eustace Smith. He put out the crook of his whip and drew it over to him. 'Ten thousand crocodiles! There is my name in it. Sampson Trampleasure, of Falmouth, Solicitor. No! that is my father. Last will and testament of James Strange, of Bahia, Brazil! Why, that's a kinsman of ours. My grandmother was a Strange. How the devil came this into your hands?'

Mr. Battishill looked at Herring. Herring was disconcerted. The surprise and indignation caused by the intrusion and insolence of the young man had prevented him from recollecting to fold up and put away the document.

' Writing to one trustee,' said young Tramplara, taking up the letter, 'and in duty bound about to write to the other when interrupted by me. I will save you the trouble. But how came this into your hands? Will you answer me that?'

'I have already told you, Mr. Sampson, that there has been a death in the house. An unfortunate and melancholy accident took place last Friday, a carriage was upset near this house, and a strange gentleman killed. He was brought here, and has been buried to-day.'

'That was Mr. James Strange?'

'It was. He was a gentleman who, according to his daughter's account, had lived many years in Brazil as a diamond merchant.'

'I know that. He was my father's first cousin; consequently he was—blowed if I know—but cousin of some sort, and about the only relative on that side I had. What did he die worth?'

'That will be for your father to ascertain,' said Herring.

'It seems to me a most extraordinary thing to find a will of one not even remotely belonging to you lying on your table where it might be torn to light pipes with.'

'The reason is very simple,' said Herring. 'Mr. Battishill and I knew nothing about Mr. Strange, and his daughter seemed to be equally in the dark about his relatives.'

'What, is that pretty girl in the garden along of Miss Cicely his daughter?'

'That young lady is his daughter. Mr.

Battishill and I examined the papers of the deceased. Most were in Portuguese, which we were unable to read. From the will we gathered who were the trustees and guardians of the lady. That was what we sought, and that was what we have ascertained.'

'Well, this is a rise,' said young Tramplara. 'This is like going out after a partridge and starting a pheasant. But never mind. I keep my game in my eye. You will have to unburthen your pockets, Battishill, old boy!'

'Has the sea broken in on Polpluggan?' asked Mr. Battishill dolefully. He knew well enough that the visit did not relate to Polpluggan, but he tried to put off the worst.

'Polpluggan,' said the young man, with a touch of melancholy in his voice; 'Polpluggan is swamped outright. The mighty Atlantic has got on top of him, and is pouring himself down his throat. There ain't no more pumping to be done there, more's the pity.'

'No more calls, then, on the shareholders?'

'No.'

'Nor dividends either?'

'Oh dear no. What's lost is lost. Polpluggan was a very pretty thing; but there— his day is over, more's the pity.' He sighed. 'He was as fine a fellow in the way of tin as you might wish to look on. But with the

best intentions you can't go after a lode into
the bowels of the stormy deep. The public
don't like it; and when you call on them
every month to pump out the ocean, they
turn unpleasant, and apply live coals to your
tail and make you squeak. No—Polpluggan
is no more.' Then with a boisterous laugh
and a slap on the table, 'Never mind the
death of Polpluggan, old chap. We aren't
seen the end of Cornish mining yet. There are
many more, bigger nor Polpluggan, looming in
the future. But that's neither here nor there.
What I've come about is the interest that
ought to have been paid last Lady.'

'It has been a bad time, Mr. Sampson.
The sheep have been cawed, and I have done
all I could to save them. It was the rain last
fall and all the winter that did it. I kept
them off the clay land, and I tried every
remedy I could think of. The last, and that
which promised best, was bruised box leaves.
We cut off all our box borders in the garden,
used every green sprout and leaf, but it was
not sufficient. The poor beasts picked up a
little on it, but no lasting cure was effected,
and they just rotted away.'

'Oh, blow the sheep!' said young Tramplara, coarsely. 'It ain't them I want, but
the money.'

'But I have not got the money,' sighed Mr. Battishill. 'If I could have sold my sheep I could have paid. But not only so. The farmer at Upaver has lost his sheep as well, and several bullocks to boot, so that he has fallen behind with his rent. It is a very extraordinary thing that my sheep should get cawed, for I have never known such a thing happen before in this high land. Down in the valley on the clay is another matter. But you never saw any of that blue grass on my upland, which is the signal Nature throws out that no sheep are to draw nigh. It has always been said that peat——'

'Faith! it is only a matter of time. A year or two don't matter particularly,' said Sampson Tramplara, 'sooner or later scatt you go. If you chose to speculate you must look out for the consequences. You ought to know what mining means at your age. You don't think to walk over a bog, and not get stogged.'

'Your own father urged me on. But for him I would have had nothing to do with Polpluggan.'

'Nor with draining either?'

'That was my blunder. Polpluggan was the pit down which I fell hopelessly, and your father led me to the brink and pushed me over.'

'There [are plenty to keep you company, if that be a consolation,' said young Sampson. 'Now it has just, come to this. You don't suppose my father hasn't lost also in Polpluggan, do y'. I can tell you he has—a brave bit of money too. He wants his money as much as you do; and he will have it too.'

'You must have patience ; all seasons are not bad.'

'But if you nip your fingers you squeak. My father is nipped pretty tight, all along of Polpluggan. You see he has another mine in view, and it wants capital to get that floated.'

'Look here,' said Mr. Battishill, desperately. 'If it comes to that, and he wants another mine to start upon, let him come to me. I will put him upon a lode, a real lode, and I stake my life there is silver lead, and plenty of it, at Upaver.'

'That won't do,' said Tramplara. 'It isn't what comes out of a mine that makes it pay, but what is put into it. You don't understand these things, or you would never have gone head over heels down Polpluggan. There is nothing to be had from you, so I don't mind saying it. And you are an old friend, and are sucked dry, and about to be turned inside out.'

'There is no water that can drown my mine.'

'More is the pity. It is just the water that makes it pay. But come! It is too late for you to learn the alphabet of mining.'

The bottle of sherry that had been purchased for the funeral was on the table, along with some glasses. Without invitation the young man poured out and drank.

'There's sixty pounds goes home in my pocket, or it don't. And if it don't, worse luck for you.' He put his hand to the bottle. Herring drew the decanter from his reach.

'What do you mean?' asked Tramplara. 'Give me the sherry this moment.'

'You have been drinking before coming here,' said Herring, 'and you shall not further insult Mr. Battishill by becoming drunk in his presence.'

'What is that?' shouted young Sampson. 'Hey! what a moral man we have here. All for total abstinence, I presume.'

He jumped up, whip in hand, and switched the whip two or three times before him; then, looking Herring full in the face, with an insolent smirk on his lips, clapped his hat on one side of his head, and planted himself before him with legs astride, his left hand on his hip, and the right hand brandishing the whip.

Instantly Herring twisted the whip out of his hand, and knocked his hat off his head with it, across the hall. Then he handed him the whip again, coolly, in a manner that meant, 'Touch me with it, if you dare.'

Tramplara's face became mottled.

'Thank you, Mr. Herring, thank you.' said Cicely, who entered at that moment with Mirelle. Her cheeks were prettily dimpled, the brightest colour glowed in her face, and her eyes danced with delight.

Tramplara drew back, grasping the whip by the middle, clenching his teeth, and looking quickly from one to another in the group.

'Come into the little drawing-room.' said Mirelle, composedly, 'I dislike being present at vulgar brawls. These two young men have forgotten themselves; perhaps next they will proceed to box, which is a disgusting sight.'

'Stay one moment,' said young Sampson. 'Ladies. you must hear the truth at once. Miss Strange is my cousin. My father is her guardian. She shall not remain in this house any longer. I will take her away with me to Launceston, where my mother and sister will receive her. I have just read her father's will. It is all right, ain't it, Mr. Battishill? Besides, this house is not likely to be able to afford her hospitality and shelter any more. Is it not so, Mr. Battishill? So pack up your duds, missie, and be ready to start to-morrow. I will bring a chaise out of Okehampton.'

'I am not going with you,' answered Mirelle, coldly, and without looking at him.

'Oh, ain't you, though? I am your cousin, Miss Strange, and am come to fetch you away.'

'I know nothing about you,' said Mirelle with perfect composure. 'You are not my cousin. I am not Miss Strange. I am the Countess Mirelle Garcia de Cantalejo.'

'You have had your answer,' said Herring to the young man. Then, turning to the ladies, 'Now, Countess, and you, Miss Battishill, I must ask to withdraw. I want a word myself with this—person.'

Cicely smiled at him, and drew Mirelle away.

Herring watched them depart, but his eyes were upon Mirelle, not Cicely.

Then, going to the table, he drew a cheque book from his pocket, and wrote on it an order for sixty pounds, payable to Mr. Battishill.

'Will you kindly endorse this, sir?' he asked of the old gentleman.

Mr. Battishill, hardly comprehending his purpose, complied.

'Now,' said Herring to young Sampson Tramplara, 'take this, and write out at once a receipt to Mr. Battishill.'

'I refuse it,' said Sampson, sullenly. 'How am I to know that you have so much money in the bank, and how do I know that your cheque will not be dishonoured?'

Herring pointed to the little black ruler.

'You will sign the receipt at once, or I will break this ruler across your head.'

Tramplara made no further remonstrance. With a hand that shook partly with anger and partly with fear, he complied.

'Very well,' said Herring, 'now go. Pick up your hat, it is in the corner, and take yourself off.'

Tramplara sulkily obeyed. When he reached the door he turned, his face white, his hands quivering with passion.

'The time will come, Mr. Herring, when it will be in my power to repay you this, and then, by God, I swear——'

'What do you swear?' Herring held up the black ruler.

Tramplara shut the door, and was gone.

CHAPTER VIII.

CICELY.

WHEN John Herring turned to look at Mr. Battishill, he found the old gentleman fallen back in his chair, his face distorted, and scarcely conscious. He saw at once what had happened. The excitement had brought on a stroke.

Herring went into the kitchen and called the maid.

'Make no noise; help me.' She assisted him to remove the master upstairs. He sent her for the doctor, and then tapped at the door of the parlour that he might break the news to Cicely.

Two days later, Mr. Battishill was sitting up in his own room, decidedly on the mend. The attack had been slight, nevertheless it was a seizure, a first—and such are warnings of others in store. Cicely came down into the hall to meet Herring, who had walked up to West Wyke from Zeal, where he was staying. She went up to him, and he noticed that there were tears in her eyes.

'Mr. Herring,' she said, 'my father is better. I am glad to have a moment in which I can leave him and speak with you alone.'

'I am entirely at your service,' he said.

She looked into his eyes with her frank, bright smile—a luminous smile that flickered through a veil of tears.

'I know that perfectly, Mr. Herring, and have no scruple in making use of you. Here you have remained in our neighbourhood, instead of going on your way about your own concerns; you have spent the greater part of every day with us, instead of seeking to amuse yourself—all because you knew that your assistance was needed. That is not the way with many young men. Another in your place would have taken his valise and gone by the next coach after the accident, and left Mirelle to shift for herself. You have been everything that is kind and considerate to Mirelle—I beg her pardon—the Countess Garcia.' A smile twinkled in her pleasant face. 'And this emboldens me to appeal to you in my trouble.'

Herring was about to protest his own readiness, but she put up her hand to stop him, and went on:—

'You have been foolishly generous, Mr. Herring. You have advanced sixty pounds to my father, to stave off the ruin that is impending. It is of no use. Do not venture to do this again. You ought not to have done it even once. However, let me clear off the debt in part immediately. I have butter money—not the entire sum, not even a half.'

'Dear Miss Battishill, I will not take it.'

'Let us understand each other,' she said; 'do not interrupt me. I have had a little battle with myself upstairs before I could nerve myself to meet you. I do not know why it is that gentlefolks shrink from speaking of money matters one with another. Now I am wound up, and can go on ticking, but if you say a word, it is like putting a feather among the wheels, it arrests the movements, and the clock ceases. What I have to say must be said. Mr. Herring, it will not do to lend us money, we are hopelessly involved to the Trampleasures. Nothing that you can do will save us, without involving you in our disasters. My dear father has relied on the hereditary wisdom of the Battishills,' she looked up at the stained glass in the window, and the pretty dimple came in her rosy cheek. 'Those heraldic owls have done us harm.

They have bred in our hearts the belief that
Wisdom went with the cognizances, and had
set up her temple at West Wyke. My dear
father always supposed that he was about to
make his fortune by the application of the
hereditary wisdom to the development of the
resources of the property, or else in speculations in mines. Alas! an owl can see in the
dark, but not even one of our owls in the
darkness that envelops Cornish mining. My
father was led on by Mr. Trampleasure, who
flattered him by appealing to his judgment
in various matters, and now we are dipped
past recovery. The Tramplaras will take
from us everything—the dear old house, our
moors, our little farms. I have foreseen this
for some time, and I have known that it is
inevitable. Sooner or later the crash must
come, and it is better that it should come
now, rather than later when my father will be
less able to bear it.'

Herring made another effort to interrupt.

'No,' she said again, with a faint smile,
'let me go on ticking. You have advanced
my father sixty pounds. Next Michaelmas
he will have to meet another demand for a
larger amount. There are thousands of pounds
owing to Mr. Trampleasure, of which this is
the interest. He may call in that debt at

any time, and then—how are we to meet it?
All the money my father borrowed is gone
without having been of the smallest advantage
to us—gone in unfortunate ventures which
have engulfed everything. The dear old man
would do the same thing to-morrow if he
were able. He is now full of the notion that
he has discovered a silver lead mine at Upaver, and he may try to persuade you to
embark in it. Do not be persuaded. Do not
listen to him. Nothing that my father touches
ever succeeds. As long as I can remember
he has been on the point of making a fortune, but has invariably missed the point, and
fallen after each venture into deeper disaster.'

' I have been to Upaver. I walked there
yesterday, and saw what had been brought
up. There is silver lead there, of that I am
certain.'

' Have nothing to do with it,' said Cicely.
' Fortune's wheel has been on the turn for
the Battishills for some time, and always
downwards. Promise me to banish Upaver
from your mind. Promise me not to put
your money into it.'

' I have no money to put in.'

' And never, never again lend my father
money—or me, however earnestly I may beg
for it. It is of no good; we must go down,

down, down. Most of us small Devon gentry
are like buoys moored to a sandbank. Every
wave goes over our heads. We are never
wholly above water. After a while the canker
gets into our hearts; we break away from our
sandbank, and drift away—away into the vast
unknown. We Battishills are about to drift;
decay has set in. Nothing but a miracle can
save us, and the age of miracles is over.
There, take my butter-money, it consists of
eighteen pounds, no more; I shall, however,
be able to pay you two pounds in a fortnight,
and you shall have the rest, if I can possibly
manage it, next year. I cannot promise an
earlier payment. Take it.'

Herring drew back his hand.

'Take it,' said Cicely. 'It is stocking
money. An old stocking is the surest of
banks; it never breaks.'

'No,' said Herring, 'you want the money.
I am not a rich man, by any means, but I am
not so hard pinched that I cannot lend a
trifle. You will hurt me if you refuse the
loan.'

'I said to myself when I came down that
we should fight,' said Cicely; 'but I will not
suffer you to conquer me. Do you not understand that I have pride, and that it is the
part of a gallant gentleman to humour it?'

'Give me the money,' said Herring. 'One thing, however, I will not promise. You asked me never to listen to you again if you begged a loan. This money and more will always be at your service on an emergency.'

'That is settled,' said Cicely with a sigh of relief.

'Now we come to a second matter; again I appeal to your good nature. Look at this letter. My father has received it from Mr. Trampleasure, requesting him immediately to bring his ward—Miss Strange as he calls her—to Launceston, along with her boxes and her father's papers. The will must be proved and an inventory of goods taken for probate. Mr. Trampleasure does not offer to come for Mirelle himself, he expects my father to conduct her to Launceston; he knows that the demands he makes on my father must be complied with. Now it is out of the question that the dear old man should take this journey in his present condition of health, and I dare not leave him. There is no one we can trust except yourself. It is true I might write and say that my father is ill and unable to travel; then Mr. Trampleasure would be forced to come himself, but I dread an interview between my father and the man who has ruined him. In his present weak state and partial convalescence, it would

not be wise. The doctor says he must be kept
from everything liable to excite him. So I
fall back on you. I told you that I knew you
were ready to do whatever is kind, and because
I know this, I make no scruple in using you.
Was I not right?'

'I will do what you wish—gladly.'

'And,' said Cicely, hesitating and colouring,
' as you return on your way to Exeter, you
will call on us again? You cheer my father,
who quite counts on your visits, and, I am not
ashamed to confess it, I want advice. There
is no one in this neighbourhood I can speak
with on these matters. Accident or Providence
—I believe the latter—has brought you here,
and made you a welcome guest, and has constituted you almost the confessor and adviser
of the house.'

'I will certainly see you again.'

' By the time you return an answer will
have arrived from Avranches, and we shall
then know whether Mirelle will have another
protector, or must be left to the uncontrolled
disposal of the Tramplaras.'

'Yes,' said Herring impetuously, ' if only
for that I must return. It is too dreadful to
think that she who has been accustomed to the
purest and most refined surroundings should
be thrust into association with persons like Mr.

Tramplara and his son, and that her property should be intrusted to a man who plays ducks and drakes with all the money that he gets a chance of fingering.'

'I am glad you feel warmly in this matter,' said Cicely, laying a slight touch of sarcasm on the words 'feel warmly.' 'Mirelle will apparently need protector, confessor, and adviser as much as we, if not more so.'

'She is so helpless, so solitary,' explained Herring.

'By the way, chivalrous defender of unprotected maidens,' said Cicely, brightening up, 'you come to us like the mysterious knight in a romance, we know not whence, nor whither you go. It shows how utterly selfish we have been, how centred in our own troubles, that no one has cared to inquire whether you too have troubles, and whether you are alone in the world.'

Herring smiled. 'There is no mystery about me ; I am plain John Herring, nothing more. I eat, I grow, I sleep, I talk. Troubles! —no, I have none. Alone!—well, yes, that I am. You and the Countess I find acting in tragedies, but my part hitherto has been in a farce?'

'And you so little regard your good luck that you offer it to the first girl you meet.'

' What do you mean?'

' Only the sprig of white heath,' said Cicely, laughing.

Next day Mirelle left West Wyke in company with John Herring in an open caleche. Cicely parted with her in a friendly manner, but without great cordiality. The coldness and pride of Mirelle repelled her, and she did not like her contemptuous treatment of Herring. Yet—strange mystery that the female heart is—she would have liked it quite as little had Mirelle gratefully accepted his services.

She resented also her want of tenderness towards her father. Cicely could not understand it. But then she had been brought up with her father, knew him, respected even his weaknesses, and loved his many virtues. She was unable to understand that a like great love could not grow out of the acquaintanceship of ten days, passed in coaches, steam-packet, and hotels. She judged Mirelle more harshly than justly. That is, she judged her as one woman judges another. As Mirelle was driven away Cicely turned back towards the house, saying, ' She is an icicle ; she freezes my blood.'

Herring turned to Mirelle and said, ' How kind, and good, and simple Miss Battishill is.'

' I have never before seen such red cheeks,' answered Mirelle. ' Do you think she paints?'

CHAPTER IX.

DOLBEARE.

A BRIGHT day, with a few fleecy clouds drift-ing before a west wind. A sky bright as that which overarches a young heart. The pros-pect as smiling as that which opens before youth. Barriers bathed in sunlight and indis-tinct in haze. Clouds without threat of rain casting cobalt-blue shadows.

The wild range of Dartmoor rose into peaks, with gullies seaming their sides, down which the Taw and the Ockments rushed foaming from their cradles. A glorious scene inviting exploration, an enchanted land calling the traveller to enter its seclusion and dispel its mysteries. Bathed in sunlight, enveloped in that finest haze that pervades the air on the brightest day in the West Country, who would suppose that all he saw was barrenness and naked desolation ?

'Do you see that castle rising out of the woods?' asked Herring, pointing to some

ruins of a keep on a hill to the left of the road,
after they had passed Okehampton. 'That
castle belonged to the Courtneys. There is
a story of a certain Lady Howard who lived
there in the reign of James I.'

'I have not heard of him. Was he an
English king?'

'He was king of England. He was the
father of the ill-fated Charles I.'

'I have heard of him. He married a
French princess, so he comes into history.'

'Lady Howard was married four times ;
she had one daughter by her first husband,
whom she hated.'

'Perhaps she only despised him because
he was not noble, and had taken advantage of
her poverty to marry her.'

'On the contrary, she was rich, an heiress, and her first husband was a son of the
Earl of Northumberland.'

'Then I understand nothing about it,' said
Mirelle, leaning back in the carriage as if the
story had ceased to interest her.

'When she was married to her second husband she refused to see her daughter. The
poor girl came here to Okehampton ; some relations sought to effect a reconciliation. She
was introduced to her mother under a feigned
name—here, in this castle, and Lady Howard

did not know her.   But when the daughter
fell on her knees to her mother and entreated
recognition, Lady Howard started to her feet
with an exclamation of aversion, and attempted to leave the room.   The girl clung
to her, entreating her love, as the unnatural
mother was escaping through the door.   But
Lady Howard flung together the oak valves
as she escaped, and they caught the daughter's
arm between them and broke it.'

'She was a bad woman ; but she is expi-
ating her crime in purgatory.'

'Her purgatory is a strange one,' said
Herring.   'Every night she drives along this
road from Okehampton Castle to Launceston
Castle in her great coach drawn by four head-
less horses, with a skeleton driver on the box,
and her favourite bloodhound runs beside the
coach.   When they arrive at Launceston the
dog plucks a blade of grass from the mound
on which the keep stands, and then they return in the same way to Okehampton, which
they reach before break of day.   And she is
condemned to do this nightly, till every blade
of grass has been plucked off Launceston Castle
hill ; and that will not be till the end of the
world, for the grass grows faster than the
hound can pluck it.'

'Have you ever seen the carriage with the lady in it?'

'No. During the war French prisoners have been confined in the dismantled castle, parts of which have been converted into prisons for them, and several who have died in confinement are buried in Okehampton churchyard.'

Mirelle shivered.

'I would not, I could not lie here. I should be wet under this dripping sky. Poor men! Why did you not tell me this before, and I would have visited their graves and prayed over them in their native tongue? It contracts my heart to think of them, lying here, away from la belle France, and the golden sun, and the vineyards, and the waving corn, and the scent of incense, and the shadow of the cross.'

'The sun shines here. It is shining now.'

'*It*,' said Mirelle. 'You are right when you say *it*, not *he*. In France he shines, he laughs, he illumines, he warms and even burns. He is always in the sky. Here you have a phantasm of the sun, without power and blaze and fire. I do not call that the sun; it is a make-believe, a constitutional monarch allowed to peep out between the clouds now and then, not reigning by right divine, dispelling the clouds.'

Herring looked round at the girl in astonishment. She was echoing sentiments she had heard in the convent and among her mother's aristocratic acquaintance. 'And,' she went on, 'your church is the same—a phantasm, a mock sun. When the servants of Saul came to seek David, Michal, his wife, took a log of wood and put on it a bit of goat's skin, and threw over it the bedclothes. Then the servants said, It is David asleep. And that was what your Reformation consisted of. You substituted a log for the living body. But why should I speak to you of all this? You and I use the same names for expressing different ideas. You have never eaten grapes off a vine, nor figs warm with the kiss of the sun on their cheeks ; and by grapes you mean raisins brown and dried, and by figs withered fruit packed in wooden boxes. When I speak of the sun, I mean something indescribably glorious ; you, a round tuft of cotton wool up in the clouds, that you can see sometimes when supremely lucky. So in other things ; what you mean by a king and a church are altogether different ; pale ghosts of what I mean by the same words.'

Herring was amused, and not a little perplexed. She put him down with an air of superiority, as a schoolmistress would put down a boy in her class who had made a stupid blunder, which merited a whipping, but was let off with degradation.

After some pause in the conversation he ventured to remark, ' You will not deny that this scenery is lovely.'

' It is beautiful in feature, but wanting in colour. I could cry out for my paint-box, and spill the colours over the scene to make it perfect. My master taught me, when I learned to paint, that shadows were to be made of carmine and ultramarine. There are no such colours here. Shadows must be put in with Indian ink. I could copy all the tints with a child's fifty-sous box of paints, warranted free from poisonous matter, as also from all real colour. Besides,' she added, ' Venus when she rose from the sea must have been intolerable till dried. Your land is fair, but everlastingly dripping.'

She spoke without a smile. Herring turned his head aside to laugh.

So they went on ; he telling her traditions to while away the journey, she setting him down.

At length they arrived at Launceston.

The town is curious, perched on a height,

rising precipitously out of the valley of the
Kensey, and culminating in a rock that has
been shaped by the hands of men, and crowned
by a circular keep of concentric rings of
masonry.

The main street of Launceston is entered
under an ancient gateway. Scarcely another
English town has such a picturesque and con-
tinental appearance.

On the steep slope of the hill, clinging to
its side, was the quaintest conceivable house
—a long narrow range of gables, roof and
walls encased in small slate-like mail armour.
In front of the house is a narrow terrace,
with, at one end, a sort of summer-house,
furnished with fireplace and chimney. Below this terrace the rock falls abruptly to the
valley. The foundations of the houses in the
street above are higher than the tops of the
chimneys of 'Dolbeare,' as this picturesque
old house was called.

In Dolbeare lived the Trampleasures, as
they called themselves; Tramplaras, as the
world called them. Herring knew little of
Launceston, and he had some difficulty in
finding the house.

The door opened to them, and they were
introduced into a hall, with stairs branching
off on either side. Then a stout red-faced

man, with perfectly white hair, burst out of
the adjoining room, with a noisy shout of ' Oh,
here you are at last! Come to my arms,
Cousin Strange.'

Mirelle drew back before the coarse man.

' I say,' pursued he with effusion. ' what's
your pet name, darling? Let's be cosy and
familiar at starting. What are you? Mirrie?
Rellie?'

Mirelle turned to ice. ' You have mistaken the person,' she said. ' I am no cousin.
I have no other name than that of Countess
Mirelle Garcia de Cantalejo. I have come here
till my affairs are settled, and then I shall go
elsewhere. I pray let this be understood from
the outset. I am not a Strange, and we are
not relations.'

The old man stood open-eyed and open-
mouthed without speaking, and then burst
into a roar of laughter, which made his face
blaze a fierce red, horrible against the snow of
his hair and whiskers. His eyes were black,
with a cunning twinkle in them. His hands
were large, the fingers short and fat, the palms
very wide. Altogether a repulsive old man,
to whom the hoar head was no crown of glory,
but he a dishonour to hoar hairs.

Mirelle contemplated him with undisguised
aversion. Then she turned to Herring and

said, 'I cannot lodge with this person. Take me back to the Battishills.'

Herring did not know what answer to make.

'Pray, who are you?' asked the old man. 'Brother or lover of the lady? Perhaps a cousin whom she does condescend to recognise; a Parley-vous Mossou, hey?'

'My name is Herring,' said the young man, gravely. 'Mr. Battishill is ill, and Miss Battishill cannot leave her father. Consequently they asked me to escort the Countess to Launceston.'

'The Countess!' exclaimed Mr. Tramplara. 'Oh, Ginger! a live Countess in the house. Lord! the little rooms won't contain her. We must throw out bow windows. Come here, Orange, come here, Polly, and see a live Countess.'

As he called, a feeble old woman, in a big cap with lilac ribands and a pink bow under her chin, appeared at a side door, and with her the daughter whom he called Orange. The latter entered the hall.

'Father,' said Miss Orange Trampleasure, reproachfully, 'you are too boisterous with the young lady. Do you not see? She is tired with her journey, and your noise frightens her.'

'Frightens me!' repeated Mirelle, with perfect composure. 'Non, il ne me fait pas peur—il me révolte.'

'Come with me, cousin,' said Orange. 'Let me take off your things, and show you your room.'

Mirelle hesitated.

'My dear,' Orange went on, 'there is no help for it. Whether you like it or not, here you must stay ; you cannot go back to the Battishills. It is unreasonable to expect them to take charge of you. Besides, your father committed you to us.'

'My father has left a gentleman in France my guardian equally with this person here.'

'Then you must stay with us till he has been communicated with,' said Orange. 'Come with me.'

Mirelle allowed herself to be conducted upstairs.

Old Tramplara went into a muffled convulsion of laughter. He winked at Herring and said, 'She's a queer piece of flesh, ain't she—full of French hoity-toity? We must take all that out of her, and make good English homespun take the place of mouslin-de-laine, parley-vous, bong-soir, mossou !' Then the old man curtsied and grimaced, and went into attitudes. 'So,' said he, 'you be the gent that has escorted my Lady High and Mighty here! My son said something about you. You gave him a rap over the knuckles, hey? Serve the beggar right. He had been drinking, I'll swear. He said he had come across a temperance fellow who had insulted him. And you also, I suppose, are the party that have been paying sixty pounds for old Battishill; lending him the money—making him a present of it, I should rather say—for he who lends to him don't hear the chink of his coin again. I suppose you have plenty of brass to throw away. Well, there be better investments than West Wyke, I can tell'y. I wish I had been by to have tipped you a hint. Herring is your name! I wonder whether you are any relation to old Jago Herring, of Welltown?'

The young man did not enlighten him.

'Look here,' said Mr. Trampleasure. 'Stay and pick a bone of mutton with us at supper. Don't be shy about meeting Sampson. He ain't here, now at least—and what's more, he's not the fellow to bear malice. Lord bless you! if he were a bit rampageous, it was because he had been drinking; and as Moses who was the meekest of men said, when the liquor is in the manners is out. But the contrary is also true—and I Sampson Trampleasure say it—when the liquor is out the manners return. And, though I ain't a Moses, and a prophet, and all that sort of thing, yet I've a pretty shrewd head of my own, and what I say is worth attending to. Come along, Herring, and have a bite with us all, and see the young lady nestle into the bosom of the family. By Grogs! I've lost my manners though. Here's Mrs. Trampleasure, and I've never introduced you to her. Mr. Herring, Mrs. Tram, the flame of my youth, the solace of my age—eh, old woman?'

' Have done wi' your funning, Tram,' said the old lady, giggling feebly. ' Will you step in, sir? It gets chilly of an evening. and a fire is agreeable, sir, especially when one is troubled with a cold in the head.'

' Look here, Herring,' said Trampleasure, familiarly. ' You are not returning to West Wyke to-night. That is impossible. You are going to sleep at the White Hart or the King's Arms, that is certain. Well, it ain't always lively of an evening at an inn. You can plead no engagement, and therefore I will take no excuse. You stay with us and save your pocket the cost of supper. If you are fond of music, we'll give you some. "Music hath charms to soothe the savage breast," you re- member the text—in Malachi I believe, and he was the last of the prophets. If that was the last thing he ever said it was the truest. Is her Serene Highness at all in the tum-tum way ? '

' I really cannot say.'

' Because, if she is, she's where her talent will be drawn out. I play the bass violin, Sampson is a Boanerges on the flute, and Orange can do pretty well on the harpsichord. But there she comes herself, all along of her Ladyship. Come in, Herring, this is Liberty Hall, with no more forms and ceremonies in it than in the Tabernacle in the Wilderness.'

He drew the young man into the sitting-room. ' There's another musician in the house,' he said, ' but of him, mum. He don't let himself be heard often, thanks be.'

Herring reluctantly submitted. He was repelled by the old man, but he was concerned for Mirelle. Could she endure this association ? Was the daughter, Orange, better than her father, or was she equally vulgar ? The mother was feeble and commonplace, not obtrusively offensive. He would like to be satisfied that in Orange poor Mirelle would find a refuge and a support against the coarse father and from the brutal son.

He could learn this only by staying, and he therefore accepted the invitation, though not with the best grace.

The table in the little dining-room was

laid with a white cloth, and there was a dish
with a cold leg of boiled mutton on it at the
head. Cheese, butter, and bread were dispersed,
not arranged, on the surface of the table. In
the centre stood a plated cruet-stand with old
mustard turned brown in a pot, and a bottle
of sauce down whose sides the sauce had
trickled and caked.

Mirelle entered with Orange, pale, her
long dark lashes drooping on her cheek. She
was ashamed, perhaps afraid, to look up.
Herring thought he saw something on the
lash. A tear?—hardly a whole tear. A
brilliant, not a diamond.

The room was comfortable. It was panelled with painted wood of Queen Anne's
period, the mouldings heavy and the panels
large. The room was low. A fire burnt in
the grate.

Orange Tramplara came up to Herring.

'You have had a long journey—tedious
also,' she said.

'Not tedious by any means. That was
impossible in such company.'

'Well, long. I wish we had known for
certain that my cousin would be here to-night,
then we would have had a warm supper ready.'

'Don't bother with excuses,' burst in old
Tramplara. 'Men do not heed what they eat,

but what they drink. Cold mutton is a very good thing, especially with a glass of hot grog on the top.'

Herring looked steadily at Orange. She was a tall, stoutly built, handsome girl, with black hair, florid complexion, and very beautiful dark eyes. Her lips were crimson, ripe and sensuous. She had a fine throat and a swelling bust. Herring could make out nothing more. Men cannot read women's characters from their faces. It is well that they are denied this faculty, or the race would become extinct. Marriages, says a proverb, are made in heaven. No—marriages are made in Paradise—the paradise of fools.

Whilst Herring studied Orange ineffectually, she was making her own comments on him. She read more of his character than he had been able to decipher of hers. But he had deciphered nothing. She saw that he was good-looking, honest, and amiable, and that he did not lack ability. She read good-nature in every curve, and turned contemptuously away. Good-nature is weakness.

'Come along,' said Mr. Tramplara, 'the travellers want to peck. Sit you all down. "For what we are going to receive." Underdone, missie? or tasting of the butcher's fingers, eh?'

CHAPTER X.

A MUSICAL WALKING-STICK.

As Herring sat at table, he noticed opposite him, hung against the wall, a large pastille portrait of a gentleman in a red coat, with powdered hair. The face was refined.

By way of conversation, Herring asked Orange, who sat next him, whether this were a family picture.

'What—this, this?' said Tramplara, taking the answer out of his daughter's mouth. 'Nobody knows who the red man is.'

'An ancestor, however, I presume,' said Herring.

'Lord bless you! no; he don't look like an ancestor of our family. No flesh and blood and muscle and go-ahead there; all thinness and fine bone and whimsy, very well for show, but no use for work. Though I do not know who the party was, yet I do know something queer about the picture. This house don't belong to me, I rent it; and in the lease that

picture goes with the house, and so does a
bundle of old walking-sticks that we keep in
the attic.　Now ain't that curious?　I reckon
the sticks belonged to that old fellow in the
red coat, but I can't say.　He and the house
and the sticks go together.　You can't rent
the house without the sticks and the picture.
The sticks are not worth much; they would
not fetch half a crown, the whole lot of them,
at a sale.　There is one with a head I thought
was silver gilt, but it is no such thing, it is
gilded copper; there is a second, mottled with
things like trees on it; and there is one, and
that the queerest of all, has an ivory handle
with holes in it, like a flute, but with tongues
to them like those in an accordion, so that
any one up to that sort of thing might play a
tune on it.　Sampson could do it if he tried,
but there is a reason why he don't try.　It is
all cursed superstition, but still it won't do to
tempt Providence; that's my doctrine, and I
challenge Scripture to make better.　What—
no appetite?' he asked, when Mirelle declined
a slab of cold mutton placed before her.　'Come,
come, we must get hearty to our meat in Old
England, and have no pecking of crumbs and
nibbling of salads here, like birds and rabbits.'
He ate himself and said, 'Missie! you don't
get mutton like this in France.　I've been in

Paris, and I ought to know. I dined in the Palley-royal, and I said to the garçon—garçon! By the way, missie! what is the name you call yourself by? Garçon, garçon?'

'Garcia,' answered Mirelle, haughtily.

'Garcia, is it. Well, garçon means waiter, so I take it Garcia means bar-maid, eh? Why, there are the boys. I hear them in the hall. Excuse me a moment, I want a word with Sampson.' Down went his knife and fork, and the great fellow dashed noisily out of the room.

The situation for Herring was not pleasant, but young Tramplara relieved him of his embarrassment the moment he entered by going directly to him with extended hand: 'Very sorry I wasn't polite t'other day; but there, forgive and forget, as the foot-pad said to the traveller when he relieved him of his purse.'

'No, no, Sampy,' put in his father; 'you are out there, my boy. Verify your quotations, say I. That same sentiment proceeds from Shakespeare—one of the writers of the Apocrypha,' he added, in explanation to Mirelle; 'not quite a prophet, but tinged with the prophetic fire.'

Herring frankly accepted the apology. Young Tramplara was followed into the room by a gentleman, tall, with light hair and very light moustache, a military air, and a handsome face and figure.

'Miss Strange,' said old Tramplara, 'let me introduce my friend, Captain Trecarrel. Captain Trecarrel, Miss Strange, *alias* the Countess Garcia de Something-or-other-unpronounceable. Same, Mr. Herring. Take a chair, Trecarrel, and try your teeth on the mutton. Miss Strange is the daughter of my first cousin, Jimmy Strange. "Though lost to sight, to memory dear," as the sacred penman has it. The young lady don't fancy her name somehow, it isn't high-flavoured enough for her foreign ideas; however, she is a Strange, so sure as lamb is young mutton.'

Captain Trecarrel declined.

'What—no meat! Oh, a Friday. You Catholics——'

'Vous êtes Catholique, monsieur?' asked Mirelle, suddenly waking into interest.

'Si, mademoiselle.'

'Et vous parlez Français?'

'Assez bien.'

'Tenez. Quand on sait penser en Français, on n'est plus bête, et quand on est Catholique, voilà l'âme qui vit.'

Herring noticed the look of surprised admiration with which Captain Trecarrel con-

templated the wax-like face before him. He
saw also the smile that leaped into her eyes
when the Captain confessed his religion and
spoke in French. She had accorded *him* no
smile. Orange also noticed the admiration
awakened in the Captain, and the encouragement given him by Mirelle. Her cheek dark-
ened and she bit her lip.

'No parley-vous here, please!' said old
Trampleasure. 'No one any more mutton?
Well, a merciful man is merciful to his beast,
says Holy Writ, and so say I. Bella, take out
the meat for your own supper.' When the
red-haired servant, who walked from her
shoulders, had cleared the table, and had put
another log on the fire, and impregnated the
atmosphere of the room with a scent of yellow
soap, Tramplara said: 'Now for some music.
Do you tum-tum, missie?'

Mirelle did not notice the question.

'Beg pardon, Countess Garcia de Candelstickio. If you don't play yourself, perhaps
you will enjoy good music when you hear it?
Now then, Orange, sit you down. Sampson,
get out your flute, and here is my bass viol,
big and burly, and sound in the wind as jolly
old Trampleasure himself.'

'Do you play at all, Countess?' asked
Herring.

'Occasionally; according to where I am. I am not Orphée. I do not pretend to tame the beasts.'

'Come along, Captain, you must not absent yourself from the concerto. Can you manage any other music than blowing your own trumpet?'

'If Miss Orange will supply me with a comb and some silver paper, I can give you a rude imitation of the pan-pipes.'

Orange became grave at once. 'Do not jest on that subject, Captain Trecarrel.'

'No, no,' threw in Trampleasure, 'it is all cursed superstition, but still, "Let sleeping dogs lay," as Chalker observes in the "Canterbury Tales."'

'What do you mean?'

'You have heard of the old gentleman in red who is said to walk here,' answered Orange, in a subdued tone. 'The tenants who had Dolbeare before us let the walking-sticks lie at the agent's, and they were fairly routed out of the house by the noises.'

'It was rats,' said Trampleasure; 'women are cowards about noises.'

'What has this to do with my impromptu musical instrument?' asked Captain Trecarrel.

'This,' answered Orange; 'whenever there

is any great misfortune about to befall those
in the house, a sound is heard going through
it such as that you proposed to make. What
is singular is that one of the walking-sticks
that goes with the house has some such a
musical instrument in the handle.'

' Who is supposed to walk and pipe woe to
the house ? ' asked the Captain.

' That red man hanging on the wall behind
you.'

Every one turned to look at the picture.

' He appears harmless enough,' said Trecarrel.

' Has any one heard his music ? '

' None of us have,' answered Orange ; ' but
it has been heard by others before we came
here.'

' It is a strange story,' said Trecarrel. ' It
reminds me of the tenure of Tresmarro, not
far from here. There the house is let with a
human skull. The farmer there, not liking
the object, buried it ; but noises of all sorts,
voices, knockings, tramplings, heard at night,
made the place unbearable, so he dug up the
skull and restored it to its niche in the apple
chamber, where it stands now, and then the
disturbance ceased.'

' Come, never mind about the ghosts,'
shouted old Tramplara, ' we want music ; ' and

he drew his bow across the bass viol, making the room resound.

Captain Trecarrel drew his chair beside Mirelle. Orange saw this, and said, 'Captain, to your post of duty. I want you to turn over the leaves whilst I play.'

A look of annoyance came over his face; he rose, and took his place by the piano.

The concert began. The flute was out of tune, the bass viol roared and drowned the piano. Mirelle shuddered, and drew back against the wall.

'Are you fond of music?' asked Herring, during a pause.

'Of music, yes. Of noise, no.'

'Countess,' said he in an undertone, 'before I leave allow me to ask of you a favour. I go to-morrow, and perhaps shall not see you again.'

'Most probably not.'

'It pains me to see you thus left with uncongenial surroundings. Your position here may become unendurable. Should you, at any time, need help, and you think I can give you assistance, do not fail to summon me.'

'You are very good to make me the offer, but I am hardly likely to make use of it. I shall not remain in this house a moment longer than I am obliged. I have another guardian living at Avranches. As we passed through the place, on our way to England, my father called on him. When he is ready to receive me I will go to him, and leave England for ever.'

'But suppose he declines to act.'

'He cannot decline. My father saw him at Avranches.'

'We will hope for the best. But on the chance of your desiring independent advice, will you take and keep my card? My address is on it—that is, the address from which letters will be forwarded to me.'

'I thank you. I will preserve it,' said Mirelle, stiffly. 'For myself it will be needless, but I will recommend your firm to my acquaintances, and I hope obtain some orders.'

Herring looked puzzled. Mirelle took the card and twirled it in her fingers without glancing at it. She was annoyed with what she regarded as an impertinence.

With a crash on the piano, a shriek from the flute, and a bellow from the bass viol, the symphony concluded.

John Herring rose to depart. The musicians were engaged on their instruments. Captain Trecarrel was leaning over the piano, talking to Orange. As Herring rose, Mirelle rose also. She knew he was going to depart, and that, perhaps, for ever.

She was relieved to think so.

He ventured to hold out his hand. Purposely she avoided seeing it, but, raising her eyes, she looked him in the face. Wondrous, mysterious eyes they were. They dazzled Herring. This was the second time only that he had met her look.

'I am very anxious about your future, Countess.'

'I pray you give it no thought. My future is in my own hands alone ; it cannot concern you.' She slightly curtseyed.

Then there came a faint musical strain as on some reedy instrument stealing through the house. It was heard outside the door, in the hall, then it passed round the room and went on into Mr. Trampleasure's office beyond; a strange music, distant yet near, so distant that the ear was sensible of an effort to hear it, yet so near that the vibration could be felt. The air played was familiar ; a solemn, quaint old melody, associated with these words :—

> Since first I saw your face, I resolv'd
>   To honour and renown you ;
> If now I be disdain'd, I wish
>   My heart had never known you.

Orange turned pale. Old Tramplara was
startled. Mirelle and Herring did not at first
realise that this was the music that had been
alluded to at table. Some moments elapsed
before those in the room had recovered from
their surprise sufficiently to speak, and then
only Orange had the courage to refer to it.
She turned sharply, almost fiercely, on Mirelle,
and said, ' It is you—you! who have brought
this on us.'

' Brought what?'

Orange was too agitated to explain. ' I
have told you what this means,' she said.

' What have we here on the floor?' asked
Tramplara, in a shaking voice.

' A card,' answered Mirelle. ' Mr. Herring's address.' She raised it and read :—

' Lieut. Herring, 25th Reg.

Welltown,

N. Cornwall.'

' Why!' she exclaimed, supremely shocked,
' he is an officer in the army, and I thought
he was a *commis voyageur* for some grocery
or drapery business. Where is he?'

John Herring was gone. She had not
even thanked him for what he had done for
her, and he had done for her, and would
do for her, far more than she knew. However proudly she may have resolved to hold

her future in her own hands, that future was in his.

'Herring!—Welltown!' echoed Mr. Trampleasure: 'why, he is the son of old Jago Herring after all.'

'Twenty-fifth!' echoed Captain Trecarrel: 'why, he must have been at Waterloo.'

'Waterloo, by all the rules of military science, ought to have been a victory to the Emperor,' said Mirelle. 'Indeed, it was a victory, but the arrival of the Prussians, and thereby the preponderating numerical power brought to bear against our troops when exhausted, compelled them to retreat.'

'Sampy,' said Trampleasure, in an undertone to his son, 'I had a peck or two at old Jago, and there must be flesh on the bones of the son. The old fool has sent his son into the army to make a gentleman of him. Quick! run after him, my lad, and beg him, whenever he passes through Launceston, to give us a call, and see how the Countess Candelstickio is picking up her crumbs.'

CHAPTER XI.

THE GIANT'S TABLE.

HERRING drove back next day to West Wyke. He was not in good spirits; he had not slept much the night before. The thoughts of Mirelle, of her isolation in the midst of coarse, sordid natures, of her exposure to the impertinence of Sampson, junior, and the vulgarity of the elder Tramplara, had kept him awake. His sole hope lay in Orange, that she might prove a refuge and protection for Mirelle. The Countess had repelled him. She had not even thanked him for what he had done for her. She had treated him as a travelling bagman, had absolutely declined his proffers of friendship. Was it likely that they would meet again—that he should again look into those dark, inscrutable eyes? She filled all his thoughts. He could give attention to nothing else. Poor Mirelle! Unsuited utterly by her bringing up for battling with the realities of life. Reared in purest cloudland,

she was translated to grossest proseland.
Nursed in a convent, she found herself suddenly at its spiritual and moral antipodes.
She had spent her life hitherto secluded from
the rush and roar of life. Now she was
plunged in the swirl of the current, and knew
not how to swim. Poor Mirelle! Herring
sighed. He was thinking of her when he
reached West Wyke, and Cicely's cheerful
voice roused him from abstraction.

She met him in her frank and genial
manner, and showed how pleased she was to
see him. What a contrast between his reception to-day and his dismissal over night!
Then a frost had fallen on his heart, now a
sunbeam thawed it. And yet he could not
avoid contrasting Cicely unfavourably with
Mirelle. Cicely was eminently sober, sensible,
and practical; perfectly natural, entirely without disguise. Mirelle was dreamy, unreasonable, unpractical; her nature altered by her
education, her character a riddle. Cicely had
her congeners everywhere. Herring had met
a thousand equally fresh and charming girls;
hers was the type found in every manor house
and parsonage of Old England. These girls
are sweet, wholesome, but not piquant. Every
one knows what they are; the sounding line
goes to the bottom of their souls at once, and

all the way through fresh and crystal waters.
But Mirelle was mysterious. Herring had
never met with one like her. He could not
fathom her; he dare not even cast the plumb.
That she had a shrewd spirit he saw; that
she had depth of character he suspected; that
she was good as an angel of God he was so
convinced that he would have died for his
faith. He liked Cicely, he loved Mirelle. He
could imagine nothing about Cicely; he knew
all. He knew nothing about Mirelle; his
imagination could soar in contemplation of
her, and see her still above him.

Mr. Battishill was delighted to see Herring. He took the young man's hand in his.
He would not let it go, but kept shaking it,
and repeating how pleased he was to see him.
Herring was touched. There was something
in this reception like a coming home. Then
they got to talking about Mirelle. A letter
had come from Mr. Eustace Smith, a peppery,
indignant letter, refusing to have anything to
do with executorship to the deceased's will,
trusteeship of his property, and guardianship
of his child. Consequently Mirelle was left
wholly at the mercy of Tramplara. Nothing
further could be done by Mr. Battishill or by
John Herring.

L 2

' Do you understand Mirelle ? ' asked Cicely of the young man.

' What do you mean by understand ? I cannot answer you without a definition of terms.'

' I mean—— What is your opinion of her ? '

' I should like to know yours first, Miss Battishill.'

' That is not fair. However, you shall have it. I think Mirelle has no heart. She has been brought up by a selfish mother, and by sisters who, in their religious way, are selfish also. She is one of those persons whom it is impossible to love, for there is nothing lovable in her. But it is quite possible to pity her, and pity her I do from the bottom of my heart. Her character is as cold and colourless as her exterior.'

' You misread her,' said Herring, ' or I am vastly mistaken. She has a heart, a very warm and tender heart, but it sleeps like a flower-bed under the snow. It is a heart full of promise——'

' How can you say that ? Have you dug through the snow to explore it ? '

' I should say, full of possibilities. She is not really selfish—I mean, she is not naturally selfish, but she has not been placed in a position where she can attach herself to any person. She has been reared to love ideas, not individuals—the Church and la belle France, and to these ideas she has attached herself warmly. With us the object of education is to enlarge the sympathies ; with those who have trained her it has been the object to narrow them. Each system has its advantages, and each its defects. If we enlarge the sympathies they run shallow, if they be narrowed they become intense ; and the men and women who make their mark, who influence the destinies of their fellow-men, are those of one idea and fiery prejudice. Mirelle is self-restrained without being reserved. She is frank as to her thoughts and impenetrable as to her feelings. What she believes to be true she speaks with crudeness, because she is unaware that the world will only accept the truth cooked and sauced. She is wholly ignorant of life, more so than a child with us of fourteen, because an English child lives in its home, with brothers and sisters, and its associates are of every sort and degree. Mirelle has had no home, all her associates have been of one type, of one class, and of her own sex. She has never been brought into contact with the poor, and has never associated with men. The defects you notice are superficial, and will fade as she grows older and gains experience.'

'You judge her more kindly than I,' said Cicely. 'But that is like you. You are always generous. Men see the good side of women, and women only the worst side of their sisters. Woman is to man like the moon, always showing one face, and that serene and luminous. That there is another, systematically turned from him, passes his philosophy.'

'I grant the likeness,' said Herring, vehemently. 'But why should that other side be dark and unsightly? No; Paradise is on the unseen face.'

'Omne ignotum pro magnifico,' said Mr. Battishill; 'I remember so much Latin.'

'You would like, Miss Battishill, to drag the moon down out of the sky and turn her round and show me a desert of lava.'

'I should like to see exactly what the moon is made of. I see volcanoes and chasms on this face, I cannot suppose green hills and flowery plains on the other. She naturally shows us the only decent face she has.'

'There we differ as the poles,' said Herring, warmly. 'I prefer to see her far, far above me, and I do not wish to bring her down to my level. I idealise her hidden side, and believe I do not see it because of my own unworthiness.'

'Let us change the topic,' said Cicely, ' or we shall quarrel, and I cannot afford that.'

'By all means,' answered Herring, 'and so, tell me, has anything been seen of that strange girl who helped me to carry the Countess to your door ? '

'What ! Joyce ? '

'Yes, I think that was the name you gave her.'

'No, I have been too occupied with my father to think of her. She is more than half a savage, and lives with her old father in a Druidical monument called the Giant's Table, not far from here.'

'If I had not come to the rescue in time, the wretched old man would have killed her. I am not altogether easy in my mind. The father was beside himself with rage, though what had angered him did not transpire.'

After he had eaten—for Cicely insisted he should not go out till he had been given a meal—Herring went in search of Joyce. His purpose was to give her a crown for her assistance ; he judged from her appearance that she was wretchedly poor. Moreover he was de- sirous to see that the girl had not been ill-treated by her father after his protection was withdrawn.

The moor was ablaze with the gorse in full flower. The air that is wafted from the Spice Islands cannot be more fragrant than that which played over these masses of growing gold.

Herring had no difficulty in finding the Giant's Table. The little clearing effected by the Cobbledicks lay as an island in the moor. Their rude stone fences walled out the gorse gold and the rosy heather. Adjoining this inclosure was the grey mass of granite stones set on edge, capped by an enormous block; the interstices were filled in with moss. Herring looked round. Not a human being was visible; no one worked in the clearing. A faint sweet smoke hung about the mysterious old monument, showing that a peat fire burned within.

The young man walked round the cromlech and discovered the entrance. Within it was. dark. His eyes were dazzled with the gorse bloom. He saw the smouldering embers of a turf fire, and the smoke crept out at the doorway, which served equally the purposes of chimney, window, and door. Then he stooped and entered.

'Is any one here?'

'Here be I,' answered a voice from the further end.

'Who ? Joyce ?'

'Yes, sure.'

'Why, Joyce, what are you doing here ? What ! lying down ? Are you ill ?'

'I be broked all to pieces,' she answered ; 'I be going to die.' Her voice was hoarse.

'Good heavens, Joyce ! how has this occurred ?'

He went to the upper end of the cromlech, and knelt by her. Now he was able to see. The girl lay on the cushions of the chaise, and some of the rugs were thrown over her.

'How has this come about, Joyce ?'

'I won't tell'y, unless you swears not to let the constable know. I don't want no hurt to come to vaither of this. Vaither were here a minute agone, but I reckon he seed you acoming, and so he sloked away. Hers afeared the constable'll be after'n all along o' doing this.'

'But what has he done to you, child ?'

'He's a'most scatted me to bits,' she said. 'Look'y here ?' She held out her arms. Both were broken below the elbows, and the hands hung limp and powerless. 'I'd angered 'n ; and yet, t'warnt my fault neither. The coord snappt acause the coord were wore out.

But never heed that. You won't tell o' he ? See now ; say after me, " Blast me blue if I does." '

' My poor girl, I will not tell.'

'Say what I sez : " Blast me blue, and glory rallaluley ! "'

' There is no necessity for that. You may trust my word.'

' He'd a right to do it,' argued Joyce. ' I be his daughter, and a vaither may do what he minds to wi' his child. That's reason.'

' I dispute that. He had no right whatever to maltreat you. But, tell me, have you had no doctor to you ? Your bones must be set.'

' A doctor won't do me no good, maister. I niver seed a animal as had been mashed that hev come right again. 'Tain't in nature. I be going to die right on end, I be. But I don't wish vaither no hurt for it. I be his daughter, and he has a right to do as he pleases.'

' Joyce, when was this done ? '

' When were this done ? Why, that night the carriage were overset and the man killed.'

' What ! all that time ago, and nothing done to your arms ! Did not your father put splints on them ?'

' What be they ? Vaither can't mend no-

thing. He've abroked and tore down scores
and scores of things, but he've amended nothing.'

'And no one has been here to help you ?'

'Nobody niver comes here. My vaither
be a sight better now than he were. I'll tell'y
how that comed about. I'll tell'y the whole
tale right on end. When I returned home
after I'd a' been to West Wyke wi' you, carrying the lady wi' the white face, him were a'
lying in wait for I, and when I comed up, then
he set on me wi' a great stone, and he hurted
me all over, and broke what he could break.
You see I'd a angered 'n, and he forgot himself. I've a forgot myself a times too. After
that I crept in here, and laid me down by the
turve fire. But vaither, he wouldn't come in,
he stood and peeped in at the door. I seed 'n
and I sed, "Vaither! Miss Cicely sez you
may go and sleep in the calves' linny among
the straw, and it will be warm and comfortable for'y, vaither, better nor the old barril
was. So you go along, and let me bide quiet
and die in peace." Then he went. In the
night I were that burning hot I could not
sleep, and I opened my eyes, and there I seed
old mother wot be buried under the hearthstone ; her were a heaving up in the midst of
the fire. I seed her head sticking straight

out of the burning turves, and her looked hard at me ; her face were red as live coals. Then her went on heaving and pushing till her'd a worked herself right out of the earth, in the midst of the fire, and the burning turves tumbled this way and that as her comed out. Then I seed that her old gown were flickering wi' blue light, just as you've seed old touchwood. Her comed to me and her kissed me, but sure her lips were like fire, and they burned me. Then her sed, " Joyce, tell your vaither that I be acoming after 'n if he does you any more harm. I knows where he be, in the linny, lying warm in the straw. But I'll make 'n warmer. I'll throw fiery turves in among the straw, and he'll burn, he'll burn, he'll burn ! " As her were a saying of that her went backerds into the fire, and down through the turves, and they closed over she just as afore. But I heard her still a mumbling to herself under the hearth-stone, " He'll burn, he'll burn, he'll burn ! " '

' Oh, Joyce, you were fevered and wandering in your mind,' said Herring, who belonged to the nineteenth century after Christ. The condition of Joyce's mind was that of a savage three centuries before Christ.

' After that,' she went on, ' I told vaither all, and he hev come here and been very good to I.

You see he be mortal afeered o' being caught
asleep in the linny in the straw by mother wi'
a flaming turve in her hand. He thinks her
won't make much worrit o' nights, becos of
disturbing me. And then he laughs and sez,
" Mother be that pleased I hev a given her
summat to play with, and her be a playing
wi' that and won't trouble no more." '

'Joyce, your father must be very sorry
for what he has done.'

'He is that for sartain. All becos you
see he've a got to do everything himself now.
Afore, I did a deal of things. I got up the
taties, and I baked 'em in the ashes, and I
milked the cow, and I did scores and scores
of things. But now that I hev my arms a
broke it puts a deal o' work on vaither. Her
hev to do everything from morning to night.
And vaither be getting an old man, and not
up to work as he were years by. He feels it,
sure, very much, and wishes he hadn't a done
it now. But wot's the good o' wishing. Wishing won't mend broken bones.'

Herring was kneeling by her. He could
not understand the girl. Was she delirious,
or was this the outpour of her reasonable
soul? He put his hand on her low forehead,
brushing up the shock of coarse hair. He
wished to feel her pulse, but could not touch

the artery in the broken hand. She lay very still with her eyes fixed on him.

'You are feverish,' he said. 'I am going to fetch a doctor.'

'I say,' exclaimed Joyce, vehemently, 'you've swore not to tell the constable of vaither. If you were to do that, I'd never be friends wi' you more.'

Friends with him! The poor savage and the lieutenant in His Majesty's service! Herring was unable to suppress a smile.

'Joyce,' he said gravely, 'you must have those poor arms patched up. The surgeon must attend you. I shall have you carried hence. No doubt Miss Cicely will know of a cottage where you can be received.'

'No,' she said hoarsely, even fiercely, 'I'll go over no drexil (threshold). Let me lie here and die where I've a lived.'

'But I insist on a doctor attending you.'

'What can a doctor do for me? It ain't in nature. What be broke be broke; be it a leg, or a neck, or a arm, or a heart, it be all one. What be a broke be a broke for ever and ever, Amen.'

After some difficulty he persuaded her to consent. Then he ran off to South Tawton for a surgeon. He returned with one rather over an hour later. Then he stood outside whilst the medical man entered the den and examined the patient. Presently he was called.

'She is severely bruised, but no other bones are broken except those in her arms. She is obstinate, and I cannot induce her to allow me to put splints on and bandage the arms.'

'Oh, Joyce! if you wish to be well you will submit.'

'I don't care one way or other,' said the girl sullenly. 'I wouldn't give the turn of a turf whether I lived or whether I died. Wot's life to me? It ain't anything I cares for.'

'But I do care very much about it, Joyce. You must have your bones mended and get well to make me happy.'

'You care, do'y? Then I'll live. There!' She held out her broken arms, but as suddenly drew them back. 'I won't hev the doctor touch me. Blast me blue if I will. If I be to get well and live, then you must make me well and live, and none else. Take my hands and do what you will. You may cut 'em off and I won't cry. You may tie 'em up and I'll say nort.'

The surgeon said to Herring, 'You had better humour her. She is not a rational being.'

So Herring put the splints in place, and bound the bandages tightly round them.

Joyce watched him with her large animal-like eyes fixed on his face. A feverish fire was burning in them, giving them a factitious light. She did not withdraw them from him for a moment.

'You're right for sartain,' she said. 'If I'd ha' died, what 'ud vaither ha' done? And her be growing a brave age.'

Then, still kneeling by her, Herring spoke with the surgeon about the girl, as to what was to be done with her arms and what she was to eat. Suddenly he exclaimed with a start and recoil, 'Good heavens, Joyce! what are you doing?'

He looked at her. A human soul was struggling to emancipate itself from brute instinct. He saw it in her feverish eyes. She had them fixed on him as those of a dog look at its master—and *she was licking his hand.*

CHAPTER XII.

OPHIR.

' SAMPY, my boy,' said Tramplara the elder, 'improve each shining hour, says Paul, afterwards called Saul, and he couldn't have given a better piece of advice if he'd been paid to do it. Since Polpluggan has been blown I have had nothing to do, and I want not only to follow Paul's advice and improve the shining hour, but do better, and improve the overcast and rainy ones. You and I, Sampy, are the men to whom the future belongs, the representatives of the age, and it will not do for the likes of us to keep our light under a bushel. That ain't Scriptural, and it ain't advantageous neither.'

' All right, gov'nor. What is this the preface to?

' Sampy,' said Tramplara, confidingly, ' we must start another mine.'

' What—tin? lead? manganese? copper?'

' Better still, my gosling.'

' I don't know what you can have better except coal, and coal don't luxuriate alongside of granite.'

' Gold—the noblest of metals—gold.'

' Oh, ah! gov'nor, that won't do. There's no gold to be found here.'

' Why not?'

' Why not? Because no folks are fools enough to sink it in such a venture as gold mining.'

' You are wrong. There is one quality I can always rely on—as the Apostle says, "Folly never faileth, everything else may vanish away." If you appeal to men's reasons, it is like looking for ghosts in haunted tenements ; they are supposed to be there, but never found when wanted. Human folly is like Dozmare pool, it is unfathomable, though you let down into it all the bell-ropes of Cornwall. You can set up windmills in Essex, for there the wind always blows ; and you can establish water wheels in Cornwall, for the rain supply is inexhaustible ; and you can float speculations where you will, and the fools will keep them going. In the story of the Fisherman in the " Arabian Nights " the fish that have been scraped and disembowelled and put in a frying-pan over the coals stand up on their tails and say, " We are doing our duty. If you reckon we reckon; if you fly we mount and are content." Now those fish we are told were men. And men are just the same now. They do their duty in coming to be scraped and gutted and roasted, and what you pipe they repeat; they have no pleasure apart from yours, and they rush into your hands to be cleaned out, just as the martyrs asked to be tortured.'

Sampson junior nodded.

'What is it that Solomon said, "A fool and his money are soon parted?"'

'I say, gov'nor, it is dry work listening. Let us have in some grog.'

'Bring the spirits out of the cupboard and ring for Bella to give us sugar and hot water. Are you listening to me? What I say is important. I am leading you after gold.'

'All right; but you were speaking of human folly.'

'Human folly is the cable[1] that incloses the ore. It is not for nothing, Sampy, that I have been regular at chapel and paid for my pew at Salem. Mr. Israel Flamank, the minister, is a very good man; a sort of cedar in Lebanon, always green, and he is as soft as butter and as easy to make a pat out of with, at pleasure, a crown or a goose at top. There

---

[1] The rock altered by the vein of ore it surrounds is termed by miners the cable.

are in the world good men of whom with
Scripture it may be said, " It were better that
a millstone had been hanged round their necks
than they should have learned to read and
write." For, you see, Sampy, they read a
great deal without knowing the relative value
of what they read, and they write the first
craze that comes into their heads to set other
fools crazy after them. When there is a
choice of herbs set before an ass, he prefers a
thistle, because, as Shakespeare sings, " It is
his nature to." You may take my word for
it, gosling, there is a parcel of people in this
world with an exuberant fund of piety in their
constitutions, just as some children are born
with water on the brain. And as these have
no definite belief, the pious element within
washes about, unable to settle. When you
was a boy, Sampy, it was your delight to make
silver trees. You had a fluid clear as crystal
in a bottle, and into it you introduced a scrap
of carpet thread, and all at once the metal
held in solution crystallised about the rubbish
you had inserted, and built round it a mass of
sparkling metal, hard as steel and shining as
silver. It is the same with folk of the calibre
of Israel Flamank. Their dilute piety is ready
to settle round any trashy notion that gets
into them, and rear about it a tree of fantastic

conviction. Flamank has done a deal of
crystallising since I have known him, about
all sorts of odds and ends. First he was a
total abstainer, then a vegetarian, then he
found the gospel in the pyramids, and now he
is all for the Phœnicians.'

' But, father, what does this concern us?'

' Everything, my son,' said old Tramplara,
with sunny self-complacency. 'Fill your
glass and listen. Do you know what the
Phœnicians were?'

' I don't know, and don't care.'

' Then I'll tell you. The Phœnicians were
next-door neighbours to the Jews, and, what
is a wonder, were on speaking terms, and did
each other little neighbourly acts, which shows
they lived in the Dark Ages. You don't
happen to know anything about the Cassiter·
ides, do'y, Sampy?'

' Not a farthing. Had they anything to
do with the Phœnicians?'

' Oh, what an ignorant boy you are! You
are living in the midst of the Cassiterides, and
don't know it. Cassiterides is the Phœnician
for Devon and Cornwall. It means the place
whence the Phœnicians drew their tin; and
where the Phœnicians went the Jews went
also. Marazion, as every fool knows, is called
also Market Jew, because the Jews came there

to buy metal for Solomon's temple. You
haven't a Bible, have'y, Sampson junior, ready
to hand?'

'I doubt if there be such a thing in the
house.'

'There is, though, only I don't know where
it be stowed away this present moment. I
bought one for taking the level of the Phœnicians under the guidance of the Reverend
Flamank. Now Solomon; you've heard of
Solomon?'

'Which, the pawnbroker?'

'No; Solomon the wisest of men, and because the wisest the richest. He sent a navy
of ships with his own men and Phœnicians to
get gold for the temple at Jerusalem and his
own house. There is one thing strikes an
earnest inquirer like me about King Solomon,
and makes me admire the beauty of his character greatly. When he were building the
temple he built his own palace at the same
time, and didn't make of 'em separate accounts.
So the Jews gave profusely for the building
of their temple, and how much of that sub-
scription went to the King's house, I reckon
Solomon himself would have been pushed to
answer. He was seven years building the
temple, and thirteen years over his own palace,
and when you know that, you can guess how

the material went. But that is neither here nor there. I was just giving you a sample of the wisdom of Solomon. Well, the ships of Solomon came for gold to Ophir, and fetched thence four hundred and twenty talents of gold-dust; that, Israel Flamank tells me, is nigh on fifty-three thousand pounds weight. Think of that! Now where gold came from, there gold is to be had.'

'But where did it come from?'

'From Ophir, to be sure. We must find Ophir.'

'Governor, that won't do. You and I are not going to leave Old England gold prospecting. You are too old, and I am disinclined.'

'Didn't I tell you we were in the Cassiterides?'

'Yes ; but Cassiterides is not Ophir.'

'But Ophir may be in the Cassiterides.'

'Gold never was found in the West,' said Sampson junior, shaking his head.

'There never was any tin in Wheal Polpluggan,' said the old man, who turned blazing red with suppressed laughter. His sides shook, his white hair gleamed ghastly against his red skin. Then he broke into a roar, and slapping Sampson on the knee, he shouted, as he waved his glass of grog over his head, and spilled the contents on his silver hair and gleaming cheeks, 'To the prosperity of Ophir! Drink, Sampy, drink! to Ophir, the Ophir of Solomon in the West Country.'

'Polpluggan was tightly salted,' said young Sampson, ' and salted only with tin. Besides, Polpluggan was in the Scilly Isles, some forty or fifty miles from Penzance. There were many who would rather jeopardise their money than risk their breakfast in a rough passage. But gold——' He shook his head.

' We'll salt Ophir when we have found the spot.'

' What! with gold dust? You'll sink a fortune in that, and the success is doubtful.'

' It is bound to succeed,' answered the father. ' My boy, I've come to see that there is a pan of cream has not been skimmed yet, and I hope, if I live long enough, to skim it. There is not much more to be done at those pans we have gone over hitherto. We must try a fresh one. I'll tell you what that big rich pan is; it is the big rich pan of religious fanaticism. I'll take a lesson from the rats. The rat when he has an eye on the cream sits down with his back to it, and looking up at the wall lets drop the end of his tail into the cream ; then he pulls it up with a shocked and bashful air, sucks it, and lets it down again, and in half an hour he has cleared the pan of all but sky blue.'

'I don't see how it is to be done,' said young Tramplara, meditatively.

'You are young and inexperienced,' answered his father. 'You haven't sounded the depths of human folly yet. Lord bless you! I've been surprised myself at its profundity. And when we come to religious folly, my private conviction is that it goes down through the world and out at the other side. It is like the well of Zem-zem, that has no bottom. I have not been an earnest inquirer at the feet of the Reverend Israel Flamank for nothing. Whilst kneeling to him I have been like a shoemaker taking the measure of his foot. I know the sort of gate he will clear, and where the bellwether goes all the flock will leap. You listen to me and I will give you a parable—a mighty comforting one. There was an old manganese mine long disused, and the adit ran level out into a meadow where some bullocks were feeding. One hot day, when the flies were troublesome, one bullock took refuge in the adit, and when the others saw that in they walked after him, each thrusting forward the fellow before him. Presently they got frightened with being so far from the light, so the foremost bellowed, and the second bellowed, and this was repeated to the last, who, in mighty alarm, dug his horns into the hinder quarters of the bullock in front, and he repeated the performance on the one before him, and so on, driving one another further and further into the heart of the mine. Well, they got so far that there was no getting them out, and the owner had to kill them where they were. They were too frightened to back, and to turn was impossible. Sampy, that good foolish Israel Flamank is just like the leading bullock. He'll go into Ophir eagerly, and all his congregation after him, thrusting one another on, and we shall have the slaughtering of them. They will be too compromised to back when they find themselves in the wrong place.'

'But how about the salting?'

'There are various sorts of salting. You only know one sort. You have seen Polpluggan salted with tin ore brought from elsewhere, and basketfuls drawn out of the shaft that had been previously put in. That is one sort of salting, and I allow that with gold this would come expensive. I shall have to manage more economically. My dear boy, when fools are hungering to be deceived, they are not particular about the meat that

feeds their folly. They don't inquire if the
mutton comes of rotten sheep.'

'How shall you float it?'

'Nothing easier. Let us find Ophir, and
the Reverend Israel will do the rest. He
conducts a religious paper, entitled '' The
Western Cornucopia,'' much read by those of
his persuasion, and throughout the West of
England. I like that word persuasion, Sampy.
When I hear a man talk of his persuasion, I
feel that he is persuadable to any sort of sui-
cide. Now, let me get my truck on Israel's
rails, and it will run down by the law of
gravity.'

'But where will you light on Ophir?'

'I do not know yet. I am an earnest
inquirer, and I have been sitting with the
Reverend Flamank many an hour, as solemn
as a Quaker, over our Bibles, making it out.
I'm hard to believe, he eager to convince.
He has no idea that I am leading him on ; he
believes he is driving me. Now and then, as
the light of nature prompts, I throw out a
suggestion, and he snaps at it enthusiastically,
appropriates it, and reproduces it as an ori-
ginal inspiration. Country folks will tell you
that every cloud brings with it wind. That
is the reverse of the fact. It is the wind that
brings the cloud. So in this case there occurs

a little mistake as to which is the impelling power. The Reverend Israel has shown me that the situation of Ophir is pretty accurately indicated. It is said in Scripture that Ophir lies between Mesha and a mountain in the East called Sephar. Now, with my incenting, the Reverend Flamank has arrived at this— that Mesha is the village of Meshaw, near South Molton, and that Sephar is Sheepstor, which is a mountain due east of Launceston.'

' It is due south of Meshaw.'

' Yes, but it is due east of Salem Chapel. People always reckon from where they are themselves. You see the line uniting them passes through Crediton, South Tawton, Cosdon——'

' By the way, father, Squire Battishill told me he had found a silver lead mine at Upaver.'

' Upaver ! — Upaver ! — Ophir ! Ophir ! Sampy ! By the wisdom of Solomon, we have spotted Ophir !'

CHAPTER XIII.

CAPTAIN TRECARREL.

CAPTAIN TRECARREL was Captain only in the militia, yet he flourished his captaincy with as much pride as if he were in the regulars. He was Trecarrel of Trecarrel, the head of one of the oldest families in Cornwall. When we say that, we mean that he was head in the sense of a tadpole's head, which is head and nothing else. Trecarrel was head and nothing else. There was no tail of younger brothers and sisters dependent on the property. But then the property barely supported the head, and by no possibility could have sustained the burden of a tail.

It was not always so. At one time the Trecarrels were the chief family in the neighbourhood, and Sir Henry Trecarrel, Knight, at his proper cost, to the glory of God, and in honour of St. Mary Magdalen, rebuilt the parish church of Launceston in the most sumptuous manner he was able. Not one stone was set in the fabric that was not the finest granite, and not one block was un-squared and unsculptured; the sculpture was as delicate as the grain of the granite would allow, with trees distilling balsam, plumes and palm-branches, with the arms of Trecarrel, and with minstrels harping and playing the rebeck, the tabor, and the bagpipe. Under the east window in a niche was sculptured the recumbent effigy of that most yielding of saints, the Magdalen, wrought in the most obdurate of stones. The pinnacles and gur-goils were all cut out of the same material with infinite labour, and at extraordinary cost.

The church was not quite finished when the Reformation came. Then the King's Com-missioners paid a visit to Launceston and swept from the church its valuables in silver and gold, for the filling of the royal exchequer and for the abolition of idolatry. After the Commissioners had departed, a rabble fol-lowed, headed by one Bunface, a butcher, who burst into the church and destroyed what the King's Commissioners had spared. They smashed the stained glass in the windows, and broke the legs of the Christ on the rood, but left the thieves on either side unmolested. They extinguished the perpetual lamp and

spilled the oil over the chancel floor. They
threw down the altar, and, having broken open
the shrine, cast the sacrament under their
feet. They knocked the heads off the apostles,
and lastly, with a lever, overthrew the font,
and in so doing exceeded the intentions of
the Reformers, who having destroyed five
sacraments, and reduced a sixth to a stump,
elected to maintain the seventh intact. After
that the party rang a peal in the tower and
finished the evening by getting uproariously
drunk at the Pig and Whistle.

Bunface never again appeared in church,
for though the Government passed a law to
force the people to attend divine service and
receive the sacrament, under pains of fine and
imprisonment, just as children have to be
whipped to make them swallow medicine that
is necessary but nasty, yet Bunface could not
be induced to put in an appearance. 'Let me
burn the Bible, or break the Commandments,
or test my cleaver on the minister's head, but
if this be denied me, if there be no more de-
stroying to be done, then I'd rather pay my
fine than go.'

When Sir Henry Trecarrel refused to sit
in the church under the preacher, and take the
sacrament at the mean table under the pulpit,
the magistrates cautioned him, and when he

disregarded their monition they fined him, and when he paid the fine and continued recusant they threw him into the common gaol, and there, after languishing two years, he died of the gaol-fever.

Sir Harry Trecarrel was succeeded by his son, who suffered also in purse and liberty for his attachment to the old religion. He was convicted of harbouring a Popish priest, and of hearing mass in his private chapel. The priest was hung, drawn, and quartered—that is to say, he was cut down the instant after he had been slung up, sliced open, and his heart torn out of his breast whilst still palpitating. That was the way in which recusant priests were dealt with by that bright Occidental Star, good Queen Bess. Mr. Henry Trecarrel saved his neck only by the surrender of one of his best manors.

In the civil wars Trecarrel made large sacrifices for the King, and was accordingly dealt with as a Malignant by the Protector. Confiscation and fine diminished his estates still further. On the Restoration he went to London, and laid the record of his services and sufferings at the feet of Charles II. The King commended his loyalty, and promised him, if he would take holy orders, that he would recompense him with at least a canonry;

but as Trecarrel was unable to do this, being a Papist, he was dismissed with, as his sole reward, a portrait of the royal martyr, full length, in which the lower limbs were so adjusted that, had they been true to life, the royal martyr could neither have walked nor sat on his throne. The Trecarrel of the reign of George I. gambled away everything that had been left except the house and home barton of Trecarrel, which were inalienable. This Captain Trecarrel had inherited from his ancestors, together with the picture of Charles I. with distorted limbs, the Catholic faith, and the Trecarrel blue eyes and beauty—but chief of all these things, in his estimation, were the hereditary blue eyes and beauty.

Captain Trecarrel's income was small, so small that he could not marry on it. He was obliged, therefore, to look out for a wife with money.

Now, as has been said, nature and his ancestors had bestowed on him aristocratic good looks, and he was admitted by the ladies of the neighbourhood to be the handsomest man they knew.

He was aware of his beauty, he knew precisely the effect he could produce on the female heart by a look out of his blue eyes, blue as the borage blossom. There was not

a marriageable girl who would not have ab-
jured her faith, have adored Mumbo-Jumbo,
if required, to become Mrs. Trecarrel of Trecarrel. The Captain knew his value, and
was not impatient. The young ladies of good
birth in the neighbourhood were neither heir-
esses nor well dowered. He looked further
afield, and was caught by the handsome face
of Orange Trampleasure, and by the handsome
fortune with which popular opinion endowed
her.

Old Tramplara was thought to be enor-
mously rich, and to be eager to marry his
daughter well, and to be ready to pay for the
blood and position that would come to the
family through a good alliance.

Captain Trecarrel was not a man to feel
deeply. He liked Orange, and that Orange
liked and admired him was obvious to his
blue eyes. But then, he was accustomed to
be liked and admired, and he had only to
smile and look languishingly to draw to him
any amount of affection from any number of
marriageable girls. He looked for something
more substantial than liking and admiration.

After much hesitation, Trecarrel proposed
to Orange Trampleasure and was accepted on
the spot. But the proposal was only the first
scene in a long drama, and the second scene

did not pass with the same rapidity and success. Captain Trecarrel had no intention of
being married till he was quite satisfied as to
the sum of money Orange would bring with
her. Old Tramplara spoke grandiloquently,
and made large promises of what he would
leave her when he was not himself in a position to enjoy his money. But this was not
what the Captain wanted—which was something present, not prospective. At last he did
get the old man to name a very liberal dowry,
and when he next asked in what shape this
dower would come, he discovered an eagerness
on the part of his prospective father-in-law to
pay it in Patagonian securities. Now Patagonian bonds were not at par. They had been
declining very steadily in the money market,
and when the South American State deferred
meeting its coupons with punctuality, the drop
had been nearly to zero, for it was anticipated
that Patagonia was meditating repudiation.

Mr. Trampleasure supposed that the Captain was unaware of this, but Trecarrel was
not as innocent as his blue eyes led people to
suppose. He was one of those few men who
know exactly on which side their bread is
buttered ; and Captain Trecarrel knew further, what very few people do know, how to
eat bread and butter with most satisfaction to

himself. An adult eats his slice with the butter uppermost, but a child turns the buttered side down. By so doing he extracts from it the utmost enjoyment it is capable of giving, for by this expedient the tongue is brought into immediate contact with the butter. Captain Trecarrel was not going to eat his bread with thin Patagonian scrape over it, instead of yellow English gold. Those innocent blue eyes of his could see as far into a millstone as the keen sloes of Mr. Trampleasure. Consequently, till that Patagonian business was satisfactorily settled, Captain Trecarrel held aloof from hymeneal felicity.

The arrival of Mirelle and her admission into the family at Dolbeare were opportune. Captain Trecarrel was struck with her beauty, but then, he was struck with the beauty of every girl whose looks were pleasing. But what struck the Captain far more than her beauty was the opportunity this arrival afforded him of rousing the apprehensions of Orange and her father that he might slip through the meshes of their net.

He resolved to pay his court to Mirelle, to exhibit a lively interest in her, to wake up a little convenient jealousy in the bosom of Orange, and to give the father clearly to understand that he himself repudiated **Pata-gonia**.

The curious mixture of simplicity and shrewdness in Mirelle amused him. It was a real pleasure to him to converse with her, and a particular pleasure to look into those deep eyes and speculate what lay beneath.

Once a month a priest came to Trecarrel on a circuit through the north of Cornwall, and said mass in the chapel near the house. On these occasions Mirelle walked over to Trecarrel. Trecarrel lies, like most old manor houses, in a hollow. A small stream dribbling through the hollow constituted the only attraction which could lead a gentleman to build his stately mansion in such a spot. A stately mansion Trecarrel must have been in its prime. The great banqueting hall was of hewn granite, with granite windows and door-way and chimney-piece. A little chapel stood south of the hall, also of cut granite. The mansion-house itself is, at the present date, reduced to a fragment of the great house that once occupied three sides of a quadrangle. At the time of which we are writing it was more than dilapidated, it was falling into utter ruin. There was no glass in many of the windows, and the roofs were breaking down. Next to the hall the glory of Trecarrel was the gatehouse of granite, with a richly sculptured doorway of the same intractable material, moulded deeply, with strawberry leaves carved in the hollows of the mouldings. The Trecarrel who gambled pulled down the gatehouse because coaches could not pass beneath the arch ; but when he had pulled it down he had not the power or the means to remove the huge blocks, and so he left them encumbering the ground where they had fallen, and there at the present day they lie, rankly overgrown with nettles.

Captain Trecarrel could not suffer Mirelle to walk home unattended when she made her monthly pilgrimages to his chapel. She was always pleased to see and converse with him. He was her equal, a gentleman and a Catholic —the two qualities which made them akin and separated them from the ignoble and unbelieving around. In these walks the Captain told Mirelle the story of Sir Henry Trecarrel and the building of Launceston Church, and the way in which the work was arrested. He told her what his ancestor had done and suffered in the civil wars, and he showed her one day in the hall the sole reward he had received for his sacrifices. Mirelle was able to sympathise with the misfortunes of the house ; she also represented a generous race, that had fought the Moors, had ruled a county, coined its own money, and set up its own gallows. In that last particular the Garcias and the Trecarrels had differed. The Garcias had hung men, the Trecarrels had had much ado to keep themselves from being hung.

The story of the self-sacrifice of the Trecarrels for Church and King stirred the soul of Mirelle, ready to warm to all that savoured of heroism; and she looked on the Captain as the noble representative of a glorious line of confessors and martyrs. She fondly deemed him made of the same stuff, ready to lay himself down on the altar if need be. But no! Trecarrel was wholly free from the spirit of self-sacrifice. He would not surrender his independence for five thousand pounds in Patagonian bonds. During one of these walks the Captain ascertained from Mirelle that her father had left her six thousand pounds, not in Patagonian bonds, but in hard cash. Six thousand pounds! That was one thousand above the sum that Orange was promised. Six thousand pounds in coined gold, with his Majesty's head on each piece, God bless him! Trecarrel's tone assumed more tenderness, a softer light shone out of his celestial eyes, and he slightly squeezed the arm that was on his own under the big umbrella, as he paddled with Mirelle to Launceston under a Cornish drizzle and through West Country mud.

That night the Captain did not sleep. He tossed on his bed. He sat up and hammered the pillow into shape and put it under his neck. Then he got up and drank cold water. Then he tried to count sheep going through a gap in a hedge. All was in vain. He could not sleep and he could not count the sheep, because his mind was active. He was stung into wakefulness by the consideration whether it would be possible for him to be off his engagement to Orange, and on with one to Mirelle. It would not be consistent with his honour as a gentleman and an officer (though only in the militia) to become engaged to Mirelle before breaking with Orange. It would also not be proper for him to break with Orange ; but it would be perfectly honourable for him so to conduct himself as to force her to break with him. He made no doubt that Mirelle would have him. No woman could refuse him, with his eyes and name, his profile and his position. Besides, Mirelle manifestly liked him. She made no secret of the pleasure she took in his society. Now the only means of effecting a rupture with Orange was for him to pay marked attentions to Mirelle, and to wane in his attentions to herself.

Orange would then speak to her mother, and the mother would communicate her daughter's trouble to the father, and then a crisis would be attained. The father would either break off the match, in which case he would be free to address Mirelle, or, in his dread of losing such a son-in-law, he would drop the Patagonians and offer ready money. Orange and five thousand pounds ; Mirelle with six ! There was no comparing the lots.

Captain Trecarrel turned the situation into an equation. As Mirelle is to Orange, so is 6,000*l.* to x.

$$\text{Mirelle} \times x = \text{Orange} \times 6{,}000l.$$
$$\text{or} \quad \frac{M}{O} = \frac{6{,}000l.}{x}$$

Now Orange was of an inferior social grade, and this difference could not be estimated under 1,000*l.* Then Orange had incumbrances, in the shape of very vulgar parents and a cur of a brother. This could not figure at less than 1,000*l.* Orange was plump, and plump girls become obese women; a serious detriment that could only be covered with another 1,000*l.* Mirelle was a Catholic, and her faith was worth 1,000*l.*

The equation therefore stood thus :—

$$\text{Mirelle} + 6{,}000l. = \text{Orange} + 10{,}000l.$$

'Hah!' said Captain Trecarrel, as he hammered his pillow with both fists. 'I'll not take Orange under ten thousand pounds, I'm confounded if I will.'

It must not be supposed that Orange Trampleasure was ignorant of the walks taken by the Captain with Mirelle. Captain Trecarrel did not desire that she should remain in ignorance of them, and when he escorted Mirelle home he came on with her to the house to pay his respects to Mrs. Trampleasure, and inquire after her cold in the head and her bronchial tubes. He usually remained on such occasions for the early dinner, and spent the afternoon with the girls in the garden-house when it rained, or strolling with them in sunshine through the Castle grounds.

At these times he was civil to Orange, and even attentive, but he let her plainly see that when engaged in conversation with her his eyes and thoughts were roving, and roving in the direction of Mirelle. Orange would not have been a woman, and a loving woman, if she had not observed and been hurt by this.

Orange had set her heart on marrying him, not only because she loved him, but also because she was ambitious. She had more culture than her father and mother and brother, and she felt their coarseness. She disliked their friends. She was a proud girl, and when the prospect opened before her of becoming Mrs. Trecarrel, she resolved to make this the means of shaking herself free from the sordid society in which she had been forced to move, and to take her place, as of right, in a class above it in culture, in traditions, and in aspirations.

Orange volunteered to walk to Trecarrel with Mirelle on her monthly expeditions, and the offer was frankly accepted.

Mirelle did not know that her cousin was engaged to Trecarrel, she had not been let into the secret; Orange was not of a confiding nature, and the intercourse between her and the Captain had of late been strained. Mirelle regarded him as a friend of the family; she rather wondered what he could find in the Trampleasures to make him seek their society, but she entertained no suspicions of a nearer tie than friendship.

The jealousy of Orange was roused. She became less demonstrative in her affection towards Mirelle, but she was not unkind. She harboured bitterness in her heart, but it was not suffered to brim over her lips. The only token she gave of wrath and jealousy was a heightened colour and a dangerous flicker in her eye, whenever subjected to one of those slights which are only perceptible to the eye of love. Trecarrel noticed this, and was content. He would achieve his end by means strictly honourable. Mirelle was unconscious and unsuspicious of what was going on around her. She liked the Captain, she told Orange as much, without colour rising in her transparent cheek or lowering her eye. She liked Orange, who, if not cordial, was kind, and who proved a very serviceable screen against the brutality of her father and brother. That the Captain was playing her off upon Orange for his own selfish purposes, and that deadly jealousy and hate against her were being kindled in the bosom of her cousin—of this Mirelle was unsuspicious.

CHAPTER XIV.

UNDER THE HEARTH.

JOHN HERRING visited Joyce daily. He had no choice. She would allow no one else to touch her bandages. He was impatient to prosecute his journey, but was detained by this poor savage, who refused doggedly to allow the doctor or Cicely to touch her arms. Herring remonstrated, and insisted that he must go. Cicely Battishill volunteered to take his place. Then Joyce became wild, she tore at the rags with her teeth, and would have ripped them off and relaxed the splints, and undone all that had been done for her broken bones, had not Herring hastily promised to remain and attend to her daily, and so with difficulty allayed her apprehension and anger. He was particularly anxious to be in Exeter, but he could not risk the health of Joyce by deserting her in this juncture. He was held captive at West Wyke, held in captivity by Joyce's broken hands. The reason why he was impatient to go forward was that he had been summoned to Exeter to rejoin his regiment, then quartered there. The morning following the accident he had applied for an extension of leave, but no answer had come to his application. He knew that he ought to be with his regiment. He would get into trouble for his absence, and yet—he allowed himself to be detained. The call of humanity was one he was unable to resist. He was good-natured, that is—weak. The strong men are the selfish men. Herring's simple and kindly heart was interested in Joyce, but perplexed and pained. He had no experience of life, and no knowledge of its problems. He had never before been brought in contact with a character utterly rude and destitute of that elementary knowledge which we take for granted is as universally diffused as the atmosphere. He sat under the Giant's Table and talked to Joyce, asked her questions, and endeavoured to draw out the thoughts of her clouded brain. But the profound ignorance, the gross barbarism of her mind and manner of thought amazed him.

He saw nothing of Old Grizzly, who, as Joyce expressed it, 'sloked away' whenever he came in sight.

'Joyce,' said Herring one day, as he knelt by her, having just bandaged her arms, 'do you know the difference between right and wrong ?'

The question was called forth by some words of the girl showing a startling ignorance of the elements of morality.

'In coorse I do,' she answered; then sitting up on her bed of heather, 'I'll tell'y how I comed to know. I were once in a turnip-field fetching a turnip for our dinner. There were a wooddoo (dove) running up an oak hard by, and he sings out, "Tak' two, Joyce, tak' two;" and in an old holm tree sat a raven, and her shooked her head and said, "Very wrong, Joyce, very wrong." But I minded more what the wooddoo sed, and I took two. Then as I were climbing over the hedge, I dropped one turnip back in the field whence I'd took 'n; and the wooddoo called again "Tak' two, Joyce, tak' two." "So I will," sez I, and I pitches on my feet again in the field where the turnip had fallen to, and as I picked 'n up, in at the gate comed Farmer Freeze, and he seed me and set his dog Towzer on me, and my legs be scored now where Towzer set his teeth in me. After this I knowed never to believe wooddoos no more when they sez "Tak' two." The raven were right. I shud ha' tooked one or three or five. I knows now that it be wrong to take even numbers of aught, and right to take odd.[1] For you sees,' she continued earnestly, ' if I had taken only one turnip, I'd ha' been over the hedge and away avore Farmer Freeze comed in ; but as I minded the wooddoo, and waited to take two, I were tore cruel bad by Towzer.'

Herring looked in her face with wonder.

' Joyce,' he said, ' is this possible ? Pray, have you ever heard of God ?'

' Who be he ?'

' He is above the sky.'

' What, over the clouds, do'y mean ?'

' Yes.'

' I've seed 'n scores and scores o' times.' (Here we must note that by this expression Joyce meant ' any number of times.' She could not count above ten, the number of her fingers, and a score was her highest reckonable number, for that was the number of her fingers and toes.) ' You mean the sun as goes running everlasting after the moon ; she be his wife, I reckon.'

' Why so ?' asked Herring, with a smile.

---

[1] This story was told the author by a poor Devonshire labourer. He believed he had understood the language of the birds.

' Becos her be always a trying to get out of his way.'

' Did your father ill-treat your mother ? ' he asked.

' In coorse he did, though I can't remember much about it. Her was his wife, and he had a right to.'

' Do you mean that he beat and kicked her, as he has beaten and kicked you ? '

' Kicked ! ' echoed Joyce. ' Who ever sed as he kicked mother or I. It be gentlefolks and wrastlers as kick ; us has nothing on our toes, and so us don't kick for fear of hurting 'em.'

' Does your father often beat you ? '

' As he likes, but that don't matter now.'

' Why not ? '

' Becos I don't belong to 'n any more.'

' What ! emancipated at last. Joyce ? '

' I belongs to you.'

' To me ! ' Herring drew back, staggered by the thought.

' A coorse I do. Vaither a'most broked me to pieces, and I'd a died, but you mended me up and made me to live again. So it stands to reason that I don't belong to vaither no more, but belong to you. 'Tes clear as a moor stream. I can see the reason on it as sartain as I can a trout in a brook. I've been a thinking it over and over, and I never could reckon it right out.   Then, one night mother began to grub her way up by thicky stone. I seed her grey hairs coming out o' the ground, and I thought 'twere moss ; but after some'ut white and round like a turnip comes, and I sed to myself, " How ever comes a turnip to be growing here, under the Giant's Table ? "   Presently I seed her eyes acoming up, and then I knowed it were mother.   Then I went over and I helped her wi' a rabbit's legbone.   I scratched the earth away, so as her could get her nose and mouth out of the ground, and her were snuffling like a horned owl.'

'My dear Joyce, you were dreaming.'

'It were true—true as I see you here.'

'But, Joyce, how could you have helped her out of the ground, as you say, with your arms broken ? '

Joyce was puzzled.   Like other savages, she had not arrived at that point of enlightenment in which dream and reality are distinguished.

'I don't know nothing about that,' said Joyce, 'but it be true what I ses.   I know that very well.   Let me go on.   At last when her could speak plain, her sed, " Joyce, you belong no more to Grizzly, you belong to the

young maister." So I sez to her, " How can
that be ? " Then her answers, " You mind
the old iron crock as were chucked away by
the Battishills. They'd a broke 'n, and
wanted 'n no more. Then your vaither
found 'n and mended 'n up somehow. There
her hangs now wi' turnips and cabbidge a
stewing in her over the fire. Do thicky crock
belong to the Battishills now any more ?
No, her don't, they. broke 'n and chucked 'n
away. Her belongs to Old Grizzly for becos
he took 'n and patched 'n up. That be
reason," sed my mother, "for sartain." And
what her said be true and right. So I belong
to you.'

'But I decline the honour, Joyce,' said
Herring, laughing.

'Will you beat and break me and cast me
away, like as did vaither ? '

'I beat and hurt you! God forbid, my
poor child.'

' Then till you does, I belongs to'y—that's
sartain ! '

She laid herself down on the cushions
with the action and tone of voice that implied
the matter was concluded past contradiction.

Here was a state of affairs ! A state of
affairs sufficiently startling. A few weeks
ago John Herring had been his own master,

with no one depending on him, and without
responsibility.   Now he was in a measure
responsible for three girls.   Mirelle, it is true,
had asserted her independence, but she had
nevertheless imposed on him obligations.
Cicely made no scruple of declaring that she
relied on him for direction, not to be got
from a father never very dependable, and
now enfeebled in mind and body.   Joyce now
informed him that she had transferred her
allegiance to him from her father, and he had
seen so far into her dark mind as to perceive
that what she said she meant, and what she
meant she acted on.

'Here.' said Joyce, 'you put your hand
on my elbow.'

'Why on your elbow?'

'I can feel there what I want to feel.   My
hands be as hard as my feet, and they don't
feel much.   When I wants to know if the
porridge be scalding, or whether I can eat 'n,
I don't put a finger in, I put my elbow.   Now
do as I ax'y.   Put your hand there.'

She made Herring place his hand above
the splints on the elbow.   Then she fixed her
eyes on him and asked, 'Wot's her name?'

'Whose name?'

'Her wi' the white face.'

'What—Mirelle!' The name dropped involuntarily from his lips.

'You may take your hand away,' she said, 'I know what I wanted to know.'

'What did you want to know, Joyce?—the name?'

'Ah! I wanted to know more nor that; and I've a learned all in a minute.' She paused, still intently watching him. Presently she asked, 'Where did you take her to? Where do you live? Did'y take her to your own home?'

'No, Joyce, of course I did not.'

'Why of course? You likes her more than any other.'

'I—I—Joyce! are you daft?'

'I bain't daft,' answered the girl. 'What I've a found out I know. My elbow told me the truth. When you had your hand on my arm one day I said to'y something about Miss Cicely, and your hand were quiet as if I spoke about a tatie to one wi' a full belly. But when I axed about the Whiteface—I cannot mind her name—then you gave a start, and your hand shooked. We'm friends, you and I, and you won't hide nothing from me. Where be Whiteface to now?'

'I took her to some relations—cousins of hers.'

'Ah! we've folks (kindred) too out to Nymet, but ours be reg'lar savages. We have clothes to our backs, and tuty ground, and a new take. I reckon Whiteface's folk be of other sort.'

'Of course they are. She is comfortable and well cared for by them.'

'Why didn't they come and fetch her away when her father broke his neck, instead of leaving you to take care of her and take her away?'

That was not a question Herring could easily answer.

Joyce did not wait for a reply. 'No,' she went on, ''twere you as cared for her and did iverything for her, as you've a cared for and done iverything for me. But me you think on just now and then, and her you'll be thinking on night and day, I know that very well. It be natural, and I say nort against it. And how be't wi' her I wonder. Did her tell you afore her left how good you'd been, and how her'd niver niver forget what you'd a done for her?'

'No, Joyce.'

'Didn't her then look you in the face as I do now, and if her didn't say it in words, let you see in her eyes that her thought and felt it?'

'No, she did not look at me at all.'

'See there now!' exclaimed Joyce. 'I be nort but a poor savage, but I be better nor her. I know what be right and vitty (fitting)—and her don't.'

'Of course you know what is right, with the guidance of wooddoves.'

'It were the raven, not the wooddoo,' said Joyce, eagerly. 'The wooddoo told me wrong. The wooddoo sed "Tak two, Joyce, tak two." But that's no count. It'll come right wi' Whiteface and you in the end. Her'll find them folk of hers not like you, always a thinking and caring for her, and then her'll remember you and think on you, just as I do lying here. Be you a going?'

Herring had risen from his knee as if to leave.

'Stay a bit longer,' pleaded Joyce. 'Do'y know what it be after it hev been raining all day, and cold and wisht, out comes the sun afore he goes down, and the clouds roll away, and Dartmoor seems to be all alight, and then for the glory and the beauty and the warmth you forget all the time o' cold and darkness and rain? It be so wi' me. Here I lies and I sees none but vaither, and her grumbles becos I can't work, and when vaither bain't here I sees nobody, and it be wisht, I reckon, till you comes; and then I be that full o' gladness and joy I remember no more the time o' loneness and pain and trouble. You'll bide a bit longer, won't'y?'

'I really cannot stay, Joyce, with the best will to pleasure you, I cannot.' The demonstrative admiration and affection of the poor creature confounded and distressed him.

'I've more to tell'y,' Joyce continued. 'I've that to tell'y which be most partikler. Do'y know what vaither did to make mother lie quiet? He gived her some'ut. But her bain't no more a child to be amused wi' toys like them. May be for a night or two her sat and turned 'em over and was kept quiet wi' looking at 'em. But it bain't the likes o' them as will make mother still and sleep o' nights, instead of rooting about in the earth under the table like a mole.'

'What does she want, Joyce?'

'Her wants you to do it. You mun lift the hearthstone and say glory rallaluley, and Our Vaither—kinkum kum over her. Her told me so herself. I cannot do it. I don't know the words. I've just picked up a word here and there when the Methodies ha' been out on the down, singing and preaching, and hugging and praying. You can say kinkum kum over mother and make her lie quiet and sleep.'

Poor dark soul! Joyce had no knowledge of God, and very dim, perverted conceptions of right and wrong. Her only faith was in troubled spirits, and that was no faith, but a confusion of mind between death and life, and dreaming visions and sight when waking. Her sole idea of prayer was a spell to lay the restless dead. Herring's heart was softened by compassion for the girl. She watched the expression of his face very intently, somewhat mistrustfully, fearful of a refusal, and. worse than all, of ridicule. But though Herring did meditate refusal, no thought of the ludicrous in her request stirred a muscle of his mouth. He was grieved for her, and he was touched by her ignorant simplicity.

'Poor Joyce!' he said, and knelt down by her again. 'Poor Joyce!'

Then he tried to soothe her and turn her thoughts into another channel. She, however, persisted in forcing the task on him of saying sacred words over a dead and buried woman. When Joyce had made up her mind to anything she was inflexible. Herring was being forced into one position, then into another, for which he was unsuited. Joyce had made him her doctor, her nurse, her guardian, and now she made him her priest. He was good-natured, and good nature is weakness.

After holding back he at length, out of pity, and to humour the headstrong girl, did as she required. She made him raise the hearthstone, and trig it up with a piece of granite. He could not lift the stone out of its place, though Old Grizzly had been able-armed enough to do this unaided. Then Herring knelt and gravely said a prayer—*the* prayer.

Joyce was satisfied.

' That be right,' she said. ' Now mother don't want her toys no more. There be a stick wi' a crook to the end i' thicky corner.'

' I see there is.'

' Fetch 'n, and scrabble with 'n under the hearthstone.'

' What for ? '

' Do as I tell'y. You'll see what for fast enough. Hav'y got the stick? Now thrust it well in, and poke about till you comes to some'ut hard.

Herring groped as bidden, rather uneasy in his mind at what he was doing, lest he should rake out the bones of the dead woman.

' Do'y feel nort?'

' Yes ; there is something there hard and heavy.'

' Vang 'n in to'y.'

Herring obeyed. There certainly was

something there. As the crook struck it, it
sounded like a metal box. After some working with the stick he managed to get it out.
It was a small box of japanned iron, which
had been locked, but had been battered till
the lock had given way. The lid accordingly
was loose.

'Open it,' said Joyce. 'Vaither found 'n
the night o' the axidenk. He found 'n in one
of the boxes that had gone scatt wi' falling
from the carriage. He thought there might
be some'ut in him, and so he tooked 'n away
and brought 'n here, and wi' a bit of stone
knacked the lock all abroad. I see 'n do it.
That were after he'd a broke me to pieces.
When I came by my wits I seed old vaither
sitting by the fire and working till he'd a got
the lid started, and then he looked in and seed
what were there, and he sed he'd give me
some if I'd take 'em. But they wos no good
to me, and I couldn't a done nort wi' 'em with
both my arms broke. I couldn't move my
fingers, and I were that deadly ill I didn't care
for nort but to lie quiet and die right on end.
So then, after a bit, vaither said he knowed
what he'd do wi' 'em as they were no good to
he. He'd give 'n to mother, her'd play wi'
'em o' nights and be quiet. So he heaved up
the hearthstone—vaither be a deal stronger

than you—and he shoved the box under, just
over where mother's heart be.　There, look'y
what brave fine things they be.'

Herring had opened the box.　He looked
in in speechless amazement.　Then he raised
a tray and looked further, and beneath the
tray was more still.

Presently he found his tongue, drew a
heavy breath, and said, 'Good heavens, Joyce,
these are diamonds.　There are thousands of
pounds worth of diamonds here.'

'They be brave shiney stones.'

'They are diamonds.'

'Well, you may take 'em.　They belongs
o' rights to the Whiteface.　You can take 'em
and give 'em to her or keep 'em yourself, just
as you likes.'

CHAPTER XV.

EHEU, BUBONES!

WHEN Balboa, from a peak in Darien, discovered an ocean untroubled by waves, unstained by the shadow of a cloud, he named it the Pacific. John Herring's exploration of life was the reverse of Balboa's course; he had left behind him the Pacific Ocean, in which he had hitherto sailed, and he had sighted the sea of storms. Balboa had little idea of the extent of the watery tract he discovered, and Herring had but a faint suspicion of the nature and fretfulness of the sea on which he was about to embark. A few weeks ago the problem of life had seemed to him a simple addition sum; he was about to discover that it consisted in the extraction of surds, which when extracted prove dead and dry symbols. 'Vanity of vanities,' said the Preacher, after he had worked at the sum all his days; the conclusion of the whole matter is, 'all is vanity.'

With a sense of alarm Herring became

aware that Joyce had put into his hands more destinies than her own. Mirelle's future was contained in a little casket of which the lock was broken, and which was placed at his unchallenged disposal. The fortune that had been confided to the trustee under the will was certain to be engulfed as the ship that strikes the Goodwins. Here, however, was the bulk of her property, providentially saved from the grip of Tramplara, and lodged in honest hands. What was he to do with this? Was he justified in retaining it till Mirelle should need it, and then delivering it to her untouched, or was he bound to deliver it to him who was constituted legal trustee by the will of her father?

The conflict stood between moral and legal obligation. It was a question whether, if he acted in accordance with legal obligation, he would not be morally guilty were Mirelle's entire fortune made away with.

A week or two ago, had the question been proposed, If you find a guinea, should you return it immediately to the owner or keep it till you think the owner needs it? Herring would have been ready with an answer that cost him little consideration. Now he was not sure that the ready answer was the right answer. Life is not a simple matter; it is a veritable problem. The problem of life is the Pons Asinorum.

He met Cicely at the gate of West Wyke. She was looking distressed, and she touched his arm. 'I want a word with you. Look here.' She held out a letter.

' I have ventured to open it. The letter is addressed to my father, but as it has the Launceston postmark, and I knew the handwriting to be that of Mr. Tramplara, I did not show it to my father. I opened it. Was I right? I feared it might contain something to distress him, and I found the contents more distasteful than I had anticipated. I was right, was I not, to open the letter?'

A week ago, if asked, Is any one justified in opening another person's letter? Herring would have answered in the negative. But now, all the cut and dried precepts of morality he had learned began to fail him. They did for copybook slips, not for rules of life.

' You have something in your hand, Mr. Herring,' said Miss Battishill, observing the iron box. ' Is that yours?'

He hesitated. Is it justifiable ever to tell a lie? Is it justifiable to evade the truth, and so deceive? He had no doubts on this head a week ago. He doubted now, and did evade giving a direct answer.

'The box is broken, and I am going to have the lock mended.'

'But, Mr. Herring, you have just come from the Cobbledicks.'

'Yes,' he answered, and then hesitated. He was unaccustomed to fence with the truth. 'When the accident took place, the box was lost somehow, and Joyce has found and restored it me.'

'I hope you have lost nothing of value from it.'

'I have lost nothing from it,' he replied. 'But never mind the box now, Miss Battishill. Tell me what it is that now occasions you trouble.'

'Old Mr. Tramplara has written a peremptory letter to my father, calling up all the money that he has advanced him on the security of the property.'

'And your father is not in a position to pay?'

'I am sure he is not. The letter must be answered, and that speedily. I need your advice. I dare not let my dear father see the letter; the result might be fatal in his present state.'

'No,' answered Herring, 'he must know nothing of the demand.'

'But if we do not meet this call, and meet

it we cannot, Mr. Tramplara will turn us out and sell the estate.'

'Is there no way of avoiding this? Cannot a portion be sold to clear the rest of incumbrance? What amount does your father owe?'

'I do not know. Will you ascertain that from him, and then consider with me what must be done? If we are forced to leave West Wyke, it will kill papa.' Then her tears came.

'Miss Battishill,' said Herring, in great distress—he was unaccustomed to woman's tears, and therefore moved by them—'dear Miss Battishill, do not give way. We will find some mode of escape. I will do my utmost for you; be very sure of that.' He took her hand and pressed it. She returned the pressure, and, looking up into his eyes through her tears, said, 'You give me confidence, you are so strong and sure.'

'I strong! I sure!' exclaimed Herring. At that moment he was feeling the weakness of his principles and the uncertainty of his course.

'Go in, and talk to my father,' she said, 'whilst I try to forget my troubles among my flowers.' Then with a relapse, 'Oh, Mr. Herring, I do so love this sunny south garden, and the old house, and the heathy moors, and Cosdon reigning like a king over all. It will

go nigh to break my heart as well as my
father's, if I am forced to leave West Wyke.'

'We must put faith in the future,' he said.

'I did believe in the future till of late, but
now my path lies under eclipse.' She paused
and sighed. 'But after all, is it worth while
deferring to tell my father? He must shortly
know the truth. It is only a matter of weeks.'
She made a little effort to control her
emotion. 'You decide whether he is to be
told or not. I am not competent to form an
opinion. I shrink from agitating papa, lest
it lead to another stroke ; if however this
must be done——' She turned sharply away,
and signed to him with her hand to leave her
and go indoors.

Herring entered the hall.

Mr. Battishill was in his arm-chair. He
was much enfeebled by his seizure, but though
his utterance was not as clear as formerly,
his loquacity was undiminished.

'Mr. Herring,' he said somewhat peevishly,
'I have been left a long while alone, and yet
not altogether alone, I have had Shakespeare
and my own thoughts to company. But alas!
as Lear says, "My wits begin to turn—I will
be a pattern of all patience, I will say nothing."
Herring, sit down in that chair and have a
talk. I wish you had known us in better

days, and when my wife was living. We had more of an establishment then. Now there is only a maid-of-all-work, then we had a cook and housemaid, and a nurse for Cicely. I do not think we were the happier for having so large an establishment. I believe it killed my wife.'

'What, sir?'

'The servants killed her. I have puzzled my brain to know which were created first, the beasts, or the parasites on their backs; but, of course it was the beasts, for they could do without the parasites, but not the parasites without the beasts. So I believe that the common ruck of humanity was made to feed on the noble specimens of the kind. We, the aristocracy, exist not for ourselves, to enjoy our lives and follow our wills, but for our servants, to support them and be subject to their whims. That which the palmer worm hath left hath the locust eaten, and that which the locust hath left hath the canker worm eaten, and that which the canker worm hath left hath the caterpillar eaten. My dear wife always insisted that this was an Oriental and prophetical manner of describing the servant nuisance. That which the housemaid has left the cook carries off, and what the cook spares the kitchen-maid embezzles, and what the kitchen-maid leaves the charwoman whips off in her basket under her shawl. My poor dear wife fought a long battle to keep the house up, but in vain. The aristocracy I explained to her are the pigs and poultry of mankind, kept and fattened to be eaten. She succumbed at last, and when, dear soul, she was dying, almost the last words she said were, " Where I am going there will be no servants." In this hope she made a happy end.' The old man paused and wiped his eyes. ' When the first woe was ended, then came the second.'

' What was that? ' asked Herring.

' That was Tramplara, of course. I was pretty well in Tramplara's web before the first woe was overpassed.'

' May I ask the amount of your indebtedness to Mr. Trampleasure? '

' Lord bless you!—you ask me more than I can answer. I have borrowed so often, and when I have not paid as I expected, I contracted an additional loan,—like an owl that I was. Pace, Bubones!' the old man touched his forehead as he looked at the heraldic glass. ' However, if it be an amusement to you I give you full liberty to overhaul my desk.'

' It would be as well if I were to get your indebtedness into shape,' said Herring. ' If

I can be of any help to you in this way, command me.'

'I don't see that you can help me ; I am past that.'

'It struck me, sir, that by the sale of a portion of your property you might be able to wipe off some of the debt.'

'Wipe off the debt ! as soon wipe a child's nose dry. I said to a little urchin one day, "Blow your nose, and cease snuffling." "Please, Squire," he answered, "it ain't no good, it won't bide blowed." It is the same with my accounts. I have tried to wipe off my debts several times, but the debtor side keeps running. Look at my books, you will find .the figures show as remarkable a tendency to turn one way as do the heads of the trees at this elevation.'

'You will then allow me to overhaul them.'

'Certainly, if it will give you pleasure. There is no accounting for tastes. There is an old woman in one of my cottages who has a bad leg, and insists on showing it me. I say to her, "Betty, keep that for the doctor, it revolts me." It is the same with a gentleman's accounts. They are his running sore. But he is wiser than Betty, he covers it up. If you are a doctor of sick ledgers, by all means examine, and I wish you joy.'

Herring was now staying at West Wyke. He went carefully over the accounts of Mr. Battishill, and found them to be in utter confusion. The old man kept receipts sometimes, but not invariably. He received his rent when he could get it, and by instalments; his tenants were always behindhand because punctuality of payment was not insisted on. It took Herring some time to arrive at a just idea of what the old gentleman owed, and he was startled at the amount. He also obtained an approximate value of the estate. It was clearly impossible for him to meet his liabilities.

Herring saw no course open except the disposal of the property, or of part of it.

The estate was small, it had been reduced, and the land was of inferior quality. It was possible that the sale of Upaver alone might suffice to clear off the mortgages, but then it was doubtful whether Mr. Battishill and his daughter could live on at West Wyke, farming the barton, when Upaver was sold. To farm without capital, and without being able to superintend the workmen, meant to sink deeper into the bog after having been extricated from it. The wisest course for Mr. Battishill would be to sell the entire estate, and retire to a cottage on what remained of the purchase-money, after all the liabilities he had contracted had been discharged. He was reluctant to propose this, and yet it was the proposal which would be most advantageous to the old man.

'Well,' asked Mr. Battishill, a few days later, 'my good friend, what has come of this pondering over my papers? You have grown portentously dull, and left all the talking to me.'

'The case is hopeless,' said Herring, sadly.

'I knew it was,' said the old man, with a look and air of discouragement. In spite of his words, he had nursed a hope that Herring would by some feat of ingenuity find a mode of relief, and would assure him that the situation was not desperate. ' " I by neglecting worldly ends, all dedicated to closeness and the bettering of my mind . . . by being so retired, in old Tramplara waked an evil nature." My situation is not unlike that of Prospero—here I dwell with my Miranda. Well, well! what will be must be—

> He that has and a little tiny wit,—
> With heigh, ho, the wind and the rain,—
> Must make content with his fortunes fit,
> Though the rain it raineth every day.'

The old man, though discouraged, did not believe that the case was desperate.

'Never mind,' he said, 'the world of West Wyke will hold out my time. There is but one thing that I ask of Providence, and that I am sure Providence will not deny me. I desire nothing but to die here and be laid with my ancestors. Do you know what our motto is? You would never guess, " Eheu! Eheu! Eheu!" I suppose that was given as resembling the hoot of an owl, but it was ominous. Poor Cicely! she will not be able to carry the ancestral house with her when some Ferdinand comes to carry her off. She will take with her nothing but the owls, and he who marries her will bear those owls on an escutcheon of pretence on his own coat. So at last, at last, it will come to this, that the white owls who have nested here in honour for so many centuries will spread their wings and seek a perch elsewhere. Eheu! Eheu! Eheu, Bubones!'

CHAPTER XVI.

TRUSTEE NOT EXECUTOR.

ALTHOUGH John Herring had been devoting his attention as closely as possible to the affairs of Mr. Battishill, and had found them an engrossing study from the confusion which pervaded them, he had not been able to shake off the sense of responsibility incurred by the possession of Mirelle's diamonds. Joyce had constituted him trustee of the fortune of this maiden. Mirelle had two trustees now, as her father had intended, but John was trustee without the knowledge of the other, and over a fortune of the existence of which that other was happily ignorant. Tramplara was trustee by virtue of the testament of Mr. Strange, John Herring by virtue of the caprice of Joyce.

Herring satisfied his conscience that he was acting rightly in retaining the jewels. He knew that they could not be safely in-

trusted to Mr. Tramplara. When he turned
the matter over in his mind, he thought he
could make out the course of events which had
influenced Mr. Strange. This gentleman had
called at Avranches on Mr. Eustace Smith,
the co-trustee, but he had not called on
Mr. Trampleasure when he passed through
Launceston. There must have been a reason
for this. He had probably heard in Falmouth sufficient as to the character of Tramplara to determine him to cancel his name
from the will, as a person not to be trusted
with the fortune and destiny of his only child.
It was clear from Mr. Eustace Smith's letter
that he had not been consulted when Mr.
Strange saw him at Avranches. The deceased must, therefore, have determined, when
renewing his acquaintance with him, not to
trouble him with the executorship or guardianship of his child. Mr. Strange had, no doubt,
intended to draw up a fresh will when he
reached Exeter. As we know, Herring's
conclusions were correct. Cruel fate had cut
the father off before he could rectify the error
into which he had fallen. Now a happy
accident had constituted Herring guardian
of the major portion of Mirelle's property.

John Herring had confidence in himself.
It was impossible for him to commit a dis-

honourable action. The diamonds were as safe in his hands as in the strongest bank cellar. He believed the trust was given to him by Providence. He was a simple-hearted young man, and believed in Providence. He recognised in this rescue of the jewels, and their committal to his custody, an interposition of Heaven in behalf of the orphan. Whom could Providence have chosen more trustworthy than himself, and more interested in the welfare of Mirelle? The more he considered the situation the more convinced he became that a finger out of heaven was pointing to him a plain duty, and that he could not shirk that duty justifiably. But he had no desire to shirk it. He was anxious and interested about Mirelle. He was certain that Tramplara would risk her fortune in some rash venture. He had heard of the man. He now remembered that his father had lost money by him. Tramplara would take the coin intrusted him, put it in a handkerchief over the table before the eyes of his victim, and, presto! it was gone, and the kerchief empty. A clink under the table told that the coin had fallen into the conjuror's pocket. It was not possible for John Herring, knowing the character of Tramplara, and suspecting that the deceased had desired to cancel his will, it was

impossible, morally, for John Herring to surrender to him the trust now committed to him.

Of all men, he, John Herring, was the
most calculated to look after Mirelle's interests, for he loved her better than any one
else in the world could love her.   John
Herring being, as has been said, very simple,
thought that duties rose to the surface like
earthworms to be taken by the crows.   Here
was an obvious duty which had worked up
under his eye, and he swooped down on it, and
made it his own immediately.

But if Mirelle was his first care, the
Battishills formed his second.   Without any
seeking on his part, they had thrown themselves on him, and he could not without
cruelty withdraw his support.   He saw a
good and kind, if somewhat fantastical old
man and his sweet helpless daughter, menaced
with the greatest of evils—banishment from
their home, to become outcasts in the world,
with no income, or very little, to sustain
them ; he struck down by sickness, and she
too ignorant of life to know how to meet it,
weighted with the burden of a paralysed
father.

What was he to do?

Then a bright idea struck him.   He would
try to help Mirelle and Cicely at once.   To

do this he must go to Launceston, and to go to Launceston he must obtain leave of absence from Joyce.

John Herring was now, for the first time, opening his eyes to the fact that to be good-natured and ready to oblige all those appealing to him was to involve himself in many difficulties. Among swimmers they who are drowning lay hold of him who maintains himself above water ; it is necessary, though painful, to give each a kick in the face and send him to the bottom, if the swimmer will reach the shore himself alive. It is only the selfish man who can sing as he walks in the face of the robber. He has nothing to give, what he has is too ingeniously stowed away to be discoverable. Life is a Hounslow Heath where footpads beset every road, and, where they leave a gap, beggars step in. And these demand and take from the traveller everything he has, and kick him, when stripped, off the heath, with a jeer, into the black beyond.

A kind-hearted man such as John Herring does good to others as he *would* be done by. Would is in the optative and ever unfulfilled mood. It is not the criminal who is stung by remorse ; the only crime that brings self-reproach is generosity to a brother in need.

The glow that succeeds a good deed is the sting of repentance for having done it.

Of all this Herring was ignorant. Puppies are born blind, but when thrown into the water that is to drown them they open their eyes. Herring was beginning life. He must pay his footing.

If Herring had not been ridiculously simple, he would not have gone to the Giant's Table and explained to Joyce that he could not attend to her arms for a couple of days. Would young Sampson have done this, or Captain Trecarrel? They had their eyes open, and allowed none to catch their ankles as they swam. Herring took pains to make Joyce understand that she must be patient, and not by impatience undo the good already done her.

She was stubborn and despotic.

'Joyce,' said he, 'I am going to see Mr. Trampleasure. Do you know him?'

'I know 'n,' she replied. 'He were here yesterday along with vaither. Vaither went off with 'n up the Coomb by Rayborough.'

'Mr. Tramplara was here!'

'Yes, he were. He came down on vaither hard, and sed he were going to turn us out of our land, and tear down the

Table, and send us out without home or ground of our own.'

' This is strange. He did not come near West Wyke.'

' I reckon not. He said as how he were going to turn the Squire and the young lady out as well. He said we might give 'em shelter under the Table for a bit till he knocked that all abroad too.'

' Why did he go to Rayborough? '

' I reckon he were searching after some mine. But I don't know. He scared vaither pretty smart ; but he got vaither at last as meek he would do anything he were axed. Then Tramplara made 'n come along of he on to the moors, and I seed mun no more.'

' Joyce, I hope to save West Wyke for Mr. Battishill, and that is why I am going to Launceston. If I succeed, then you also will be safe from disturbance. Your Table will not then be thrown down.'

' Squire won't hurt of us—t' I know by ; he never did nobody harm, he.'

' Then, Joyce, you understand, I shall not return till the day after to-morrow, and you must let the doctor or Miss Battishill attend to your arms.'

' I won't.'

' But you must. I tell you I cannot be here.'

' You may go.'

' Thank you for giving me my furlough,' he said with a smile. ' But, as you see, when I am absent you will have to be attended by some one else.'

' Neither vaither, nor doctor, nor Miss Cicely shan't touch me, not by the blue blazes. I tell'y you may go, and my arms shall bide as they be. They won't take no hurt. I shan't do nort to 'em till you comes back. There, that's settled.'

Herring informed Mr. Battishill and Cicely of his meditated expedition to Launceston to see Mr. Trampleasure. He told them that he was in hopes of bringing him to another mind about the mortgages, but he did not enter into the particulars of his scheme, nor did he tell them what he had learned from Joyce relative to Mr. Trampleasure's visit the day before and exploration of Upaver. Herring conjectured that the old man had seen the ore brought up from the mine recently opened, and was eager by foreclosing to secure it for himself, having formed a high opinion of its value. Herring went again that evening to Upaver and explored the workings, taking with him one of the labourers

Mr. Battishill had employed on it. The man was familiar with mines, and was confident that the lode was good. The 'shode' had led to as beautiful a 'bunch' as a man might hope to see in a lifetime. A fortune was to be made at Upaver.

To his surprise, Herring learned from the man that though Mr. Trampleasure had passed the workings, he had not paid them any attention, but had gone further up the glen. But then, as the miner said, with a jerk of the chin, there was nothing lying about which might lead any one to suspect what was below. All the samples were buried or hidden in the gorse brakes.

Herring carried off with him some of the best specimens of pure ore, and, on his return to West Wyke, showed them to Mr. Battishill, and told him his opinion of the mine. He said that he was confident, if a respite could be obtained from Tramplara, and a company be formed to work the mine, that the royalties on the lead extracted would speedily clear the property of its burdens.

The old man was elated. He talked over the prospect, offering many suggestions, some utterly unpractical, and his hollow cheek flushed with excitement.

'Ah!' said he, 'if Tramplara knows

about that lead he'll not grant a respite, but be down on me at once if he sees profit to be got by it.

> I'll have my bond: I will not hear thee speak:
> I'll have my bond; and therefore speak no more.
> I'll not be made a soft and dull-eyed fool,
> To shake the head, relent, and sigh, and yield
> To Christian intercession.'

The old man shook his head. 'No, Herring, you will not prevail on him with prayers. "It is the most impenetrable cur that ever kept with men." No, you must attack his self-interest if you will bend him, and how you will manage that passes my conception.'

'But suppose I say to Tramplara, Here is the money.'

Cicely looked sharply up from her work.

'Mr. Herring, you made me a promise.'

'My dear,' said Mr. Battishill, 'you have often let me see that you disapproved of my speculations, as if I must be blind. But see! here at last, in Upaver, I have hit on one that will succeed.'

'You have hit on it, father, for others to make fortunes out of it. You have hit on it as West Wyke is slipping from us.'

CHAPTER XVII.

IN THE SUMMER-HOUSE.

As John Herring entered the gates of Dolbeare, he saw Mirelle go into the summer-house. This summer-house stood at the edge of the terrace between the garden-gate and the house.

He desired to see her alone, and therefore, before going to the front door, he turned to the garden lodge and stood in the doorway.

Mirelle saw him and bowed slightly. Herring went in, and up to her. Then, after a moment's hesitation, she held out her hand.

He took it, but he might as well have touched an icicle. No token of pleasurable recognition appeared in her face.

'You are surprised to see me,' said Herring, 'I dare say.'

'Not at all,' she answered. 'Why should I be? I know nothing of your movements. If you had told me you were going to

Moscow, and I had seen you start in that direction, I should be surprised to see you here now ; but as I know neither where you live nor what places you frequent, there is nothing in your reappearance to justify surprise.'

'I have come to-day from West Wyke.'

'Indeed! I hope you left all well there.'

'Only fairly so. You have not heard what happened to poor Joyce.'

'I do not know who poor Joyce is.'

'Joyce is that wild girl who helped you to West Wyke on the evening of the accident.'

'I remember an uncouth and unmannerly *paysanne*. Is her name Joyce ? I did not know it. If I had heard it, the name escaped my memory. Joyce! what is the derivation of the name Joyce ?[1] Joieuse, I presume— a singularly inappropriate name in this case.'

'Very much so, poor child. That brutal father of hers broke her arms, and otherwise seriously injured her.'

'Indeed! These savages have their ways.'

Herring was shocked at her want of feeling.

---

[1] In the South Tawton Register stands this entry under Baptisms : ' Jocosa, anglicè Joyce, daughter of ——,' &c. It was formerly a common name in Devon.

' You do not seem to feel for her, and yet she helped you, as you may remember.'

' Of course I am very sorry. I am sorry when I hear a mason has fallen off a scaffold, or a child has tumbled into a well, or a horse has broken his knees ; I am sorry when a donkey is roughly treated. But unless I am acquainted with the mason, and the child, and the horse, and the ass, I do not feel more than a transient pity. You possibly have seen sufficient of this wild girl to possess some interest in her ; I know absolutely nothing of her. How, then, can I feel for her more than I do when I say I am sorry ? '

' May I take a chair ? '

' Certainly. Sit down, and we will talk. I have something I wish particularly to say to you. I am sorry that I let you go the other time without thanking you formally for having rescued me from the broken carriage, for having seen to the funeral of my poor father, and for having conveyed me hither to the care of these people here.'

She spoke without any expression in her tone, simply as though repeating a lesson learned by rote. When she had spoken, she drew a long breath like a sigh of relief. She had discharged a duty. It was off her mind, and she was free.

'You see for yourself, Mr. Herring, that the feelings of the heart are too sacred to be dispersed over the earth, to be scattered like coins amidst a crowd of beggars. One meets with some thousands of persons in the course of existence, and cannot cut one's heart into little bits and present each with a portion. We must reserve it for true friends, and give it them entire. Those who pass us by, and whom we see but for a while, are like the figures of a magic-lantern slide ; they make us laugh, or they interest us for the moment, and then are forgotten. When we hear that a slide is broken, we ask, which ? The man driving a wheelbarrow, or the old woman who desired she were pope, or the cabbage that becomes a tailor ? When we are informed, we do not weep, we merely say, It can be replaced.'

'I hope you do not class the Battishills among your magic-lantern slides.'

'No, I know them, and they have been kind to me. I even like Mr. Battishill. He has his ideas.'

'And Miss Cicely ? '

'She is rustic and good-hearted. But she does not think. She has no knowledge of books. She could be made passable if sent to school, but must be recreated to be given ideas. Besides, I am not fond of the plump and the *ingénue.*'

'You have not asked after Mr. Battishill. If it be not too great an effort for your memory, you will recall that he had a stroke before you left West Wyke.'

'Do not be sarcastic. I remember that perfectly well. If you will trouble your memory, you will recall that I did, on first learning you came from West Wyke, ask after Mr. and Miss Battishill. I remember that he had a paralytic stroke, but I recall as well that he showed good signs of recovery.'

'I am afraid, Countess, that he stands the chance of another stroke; for he is menaced with a great evil, and any profound agitation is likely to bring on a second seizure.'

'I am very sorry to hear it.'

'His affairs are involved to such an extent that it will be necessary for his property to be sold, and he will have to leave West Wyke.'

'Then he can go and live in France; anywhere must be better than that dismal old house on a barren moor. It is best that it should be so. He will escape from a dungeon.'

'You do not understand that his heart is bound up with West Wyke, and that to transplant him from the home of his ancestors will be to kill him.'

'He thinks West Wyke a Paradise only because he has never crossed the Channel. When he reaches a nook where the sun shines and the flowers ever bloom, he will thank Heaven for having released him from his prison and exile in that wretched house and on that howling waste.'

'Countess, you are young, and have no conception of the power that association has on the old. You can begin life anywhere, and everywhere hopes and interests start up. To the old it is not so, they are without hopes, and their only pleasure is in recollection. To the aged the looking back is almost as sweet as the looking forward is to the young.'

'Then let him sit down in an arbour of roses, and dream of the past there; not in a dingy old parlour with smoked ceiling, and the rain pattering against the window.'

'I fear that he will be turned destitute into the world, or, if not destitute, nearly so; and to a broken and sick man that means death.'

'He can hardly be worse off elsewhere than he is now.'

'He will have to go into a new home and

accommodate himself to that, at a time of life
and in a condition of health unfitting him for
a change. You are unfeeling, Countess.'

'Pardon me, I am not. I know Mr.
Battishill, and I respect his many good
qualities, but I cannot put myself in his
frame of mind. It seems to me that, were I
he, all thought of being allowed to leave such
a spot, with the world before me, would fill
me, if sick and dying, with new life. I
would start up in my bed and cry out, Take
me to France; there I know I shall be well.'

'As he does not know France, he has no
such desire. And he is too old to acquire
new tastes. There comes a time when the
mind as well as the body is tired, and all
it asks is to be given rest. New scenes, new
associates, new habits exact too much of the
exhausted spirit. Have you not seen a
feeble flame extinguished by fresh fuel being
put round it with the hope of coaxing it into
a blaze ? This is not all; the rupture of old
associations is the rupture of the thousand
filaments the tree root has woven in the soil
about it. Break these, and though the tree
be transplanted from cold clay to richest loam,
it will die. Think of your own forefather ·
when he lost Cantalejo. Think how his
heart ached, how he turned to take a last

look at the ancient walls, and could see nothing, for, strong man as he was, his eyes were full of tears. He knew that with him his entire posterity was banished for ever.'

'I can understand that,' said Mirelle, sadly ; 'never more able to coin his own money, nor hang any one on his own gallows.'

'And your ancestor went forth hale and able to meet the world, and conquer himself a new place in it.'

'Yes,' said Mirelle, raising her head proudly, 'he was a brave soldier. He fought, and was killed in the wars.'

'But this poor old man is broken with years and infirmities.'

'It is the will of God.'

'He dies, and his daughter is cast adrift, without means, and ignorant of the world.'

'Do not speak to me of her. She is the embodiment of prose—pleasing and entertaining, but still prose. The world is prosaic, and she will always find a hole in it into which she can fit. It is those with ideas, the originals and the poets, who are adrift and homeless. Every gate is closed to them.'

'Countess, think of that evening when the accident took place, and your poor father was killed. You were left on the moor, knowing nothing of the place where you were, or of the

people among whom your lot was to be cast.
What if, by an unlucky chance, I had not been
present to assist you, and the Battishills had
not been ready to receive you ? What would
you have done on that moor, alone, without
adviser, without home, and without money ?
The savages would have fallen upon you—
that ruthless man who has smashed the bones
of his own daughter would not have spared
you.'

Mirelle shivered.

'You may well shudder ; I do not know
what would have become of you. But a
merciful Providence interposed in your behalf,
and raised up to you friends who have cared
for you.'

'Yes,' she said, 'I see that. I see that
now.'

'Cicely Battishill is like to be placed in
a very similar position ; to be left homeless
and friendless in the world, standing by a
father, who, if not dead, is as bad as dead for
all the help he can afford her. She cannot
become a governess and earn her bread, she
has her father to nurse. Now, Countess, when
you think of your own condition on that
eventful night, and of what might have become
of you unless the Battishills had thrown open
their door to you and cherished you, then,

perhaps, you will be able to realise the condition of Miss Battishill, who, though she may
be prosaic, as you say, is a delicate maiden,
and has the nurture of a gentlewoman.'

'Mon Dieu! que puis-je faire, moi! You
speak to me as though I could save them. I
can do nothing, with the best desire to help
them. I cannot invite them to make this their
refuge. This is not my home. It is simply
a menagerie in which I am allowed a cage
among the bears.'

'I think it is your *duty* to do what you can
to assist the Battishills.'

'Show me the way, and I will not shrink
from performing any duty. But you must
see I am unable to help these good people.'

'Not altogether unable, Countess. Your
father has left you several thousand pounds,
which are in the hands of Mr. Trampleasure,
in trust. He must invest them for you. He
is also the man who has a hold on the estate
of the Battishills. Get him to take your
money, or as much of it as is needed, in payment of the sum owed him by Mr. Battishill,
and to transfer to you his claims on the property. That is, let him transfer the mortgage
on West Wyke from himself personally to
himself as trustee for you. Then you will be
mistress over the estate of the Battishills, and

if you will not foreclose, I can promise you
that the interest shall be regularly and punctually paid. I am certain that the investment is
sound. By this means you will be benefiting
the Battishills and yourself simultaneously.'

'I understand nothing about mortgages,
investments, or interest. I leave that to
others. If this proposal of yours enable me
to wipe off an obligation I owe to those who
have been kind to me, I accept it gladly, and
if it be a duty I shall make it a matter of
conscience to fulfil it.'

'It is a duty. At least I think it is.
Judge for yourself. You see your benefactors
the Battishills in distress, and you have it in
your power to rescue them from ruin at no
cost to yourself. It seems to me that no duty
could be put in a plainer form before you.'

'Mr. Trampleasure is in the house. He
will have to be consulted. We cannot act
without him. Will you summon him hither,
and we will arrange the matter on the spot.
You will not find me one to shrink from the
discharge of a duty.'

John Herring left Mirelle, and did as she
desired. He found Mr. Trampleasure at home,
as she had said. He was engaged with his
son in the dining-room on some plans, and
they had a bottle of spirits and a jug of hot

water on the table at their elbows, though the time was early in the afternoon.

Old Tramplara greeted Herring with effusion, the young one sulkily. Herring told the father that the Countess wanted to speak to him in the summer-house for a few moments, if he would oblige her with his presence.

'See what comes of having a live Countess in the house,' said the old man, laughing ; ' I have to dance after her. Now, if she had been plain missie, she would have come here to see me.'

Then he accompanied Herring to the summer-house. This house was, in fact, a room of fair size, furnished with a fireplace and carved mantelpiece, that contained a quaint old painting on panel. The windows were large, and that to the south-east overhung the precipice, and commanded a magnificent view down the valley of the Tamar and up that of the Lyd to the range of Dartmoor, which rose as a wall against the horizon, broken into many rocky peaks, a veritable mountain chain.

Mirelle had a chair and table in this window, and was engaged on the manufacture of tinsel flowers for the chapel at Trecarrel.

The table was covered with scraps of foil

and bits of coloured silks ; and the snippings strewed the floor.

'Well, Serene Highness de Candlestickio!' exclaimed the old man, noisily, as he came in, with a burst of laughter ; 'what does your consequentialness desire ? Some wires to stick them gewgaws on ?'

Mirelle shrank before the uproarious old man, and spoke in her coldest and most reserved manner.

'I have sent for you, Mr. Trampleasure, about my money which has been intrusted to you. Mr. Herring has been advising me how to dispose of it.'

'Oh, indeed ; very good of Mr. Lieutenant Herring.'

'I do not myself understand these matters, and so I have requested Mr. Herring to explain my wishes to you. It seems that Mr. Battishill is in trouble, and owes you money !'

'That is true as gospel,' said Tramplara ; 'he owes me an imperial bushel of it. There are some persons who have a liking for borrowing, and much prefer that to paying. Mr. Battishill is one of these, and I have been his victim. And although David does say, "Blessed is he that borroweth and payeth not again," yet that is one point on which David and Sampson Trampleasure are at issue.'

'Mr. Battishill is prepared to pay regularly the interest on the loans he has contracted,' said Herring.

'But, my dear lieutenant,' said Tramplara, 'I happen at this moment to be in immediate want of a very large sum of ready money. I call on Battishill to refund what he has borrowed. He can't do it, and I sell up.'

'You are very hard. Are you aware that he has had a seizure, and is ill?'

'Can't help that, lieutenant, I want money. You saw sweet Sampy and me engaged on some plans when you came into the room. Well, we are in for a venture, and shall want money to carry it out.'

'What the Countess proposes——'

'Oh, blow your Countesses,' said young Tramplara, putting his head in, and then following with his body. 'There are no Countesses in this shop. The lady yonder is Miss Strange, only daughter and heiress to James Strange, Esquire, of Bahia, Brazil.'

'Shut your trap, Sampy,' said his father. 'No impertinence here. Manners before ladies of the tip-top aristocracy, please. What do you say, sir, about the proposal of the Countess?'

'I decline to discuss this matter before your son,' said Herring, indignantly. 'It in

no way concerns him, and he was not invited
to be present.'

'The business is Trampleasure and Son,'
said young Sampson. 'The firm bears that
name throughout the county.'

'But the firm has nothing to do with the
affairs of the Countess Mirelle Garcia.'

'Oh! I beg pardon,' said the young man.
'The trustees and guardians of her ladyship
are Trampleasure and Herring—more cor-
rectly, Herring and Trampleasure.'

'I have no further right to interfere,' said
Herring, with difficulty retaining his com-
posure, 'than as spokesman for the Countess,
who has empowered me to act in her name.
Have I your authority for what I say and do,
Countess?' He turned to Mirelle.

'My full authority,' she answered. 'I
have requested you to speak my wishes in
this matter to Mr. Trampleasure. As for his
son, I must request him to efface himself, and
not to trouble his head with my affairs.'

'Go, Sampy,' said his father. 'Good
angels attend you.' The young man withdrew
sullenly. 'Now then, Lieutenant Herring, I
am at your service.'

'The Countess wishes that her money, left
in your hands as trustee, may be invested in
the mortgages on the West Wyke estate.

These mortgages you hold. Five thousand pounds are owing to you, and you are in immediate need of the money. Take five thousand of her money, and transfer to her the claims on West Wyke.'

'Oh, ah! When is she likely to get her interest? You had to help the Squire out of one hobble, and he will be dropping into another shortly.'

'I can answer for it that the interest will be paid punctually and in full.'

'I don't approve of the investment. I don't regard it as sound.'

'I wish it,' said Mirelle.

'My dear pet and pearl of the aristocracy,' said the old man, 'I am solely responsible for what is done with the money. I must look after your interest in the matter. Why, if I yielded to your request, you would get only four and a half for your money, and I can assure you of seven.'

'She would prefer the smaller sum on this security than the larger on one more risky.'

'Risky, risky! what!—Ophir a risk! My dear Herring, I know better than you where security lies. The young lady's money will be invested in a gold mine—in the gold of Ophir! I said seven per cent., but I am

sanguine of a rise to ten, fifteen, twenty,
twenty-five. What do you think of that,
eh?'

'Mr. Trampleasure,' said Mirelle, 'if I
have any voice in this matter——'

'You have none—none whatever.'

'And if I particularly entreat you not to
run risks with my money in gold or other
mines, but to dispose of it for the relief of the
Battishills——'

'Then I shall turn a deaf ear to you. I
am responsible to no one. Your father has
left me supreme judge in the matter, and I
shall act as my own conscience and your
interest direct.'

'Surely, Mr. Trampleasure——'

'Surely you cry to a stone wall. I shall
discharge the obligation your father laid on
me with strict fidelity. I am a man of wide
experience, and I venture to think that Mr.
Herring's knowledge of money investments
is recent and partial. I object to his interference, and, but for the respect I owe to the
memory of his father, Jago Herring, I should
resent it.'

'I have no right, I admit,' said Herring,
'other than that I derive from an interest in
the welfare of both the Countess and the
Battishills, and from the request she has

made me to speak in her name and make a proposal which will benefit both parties.'

'I refuse what is offered,' said Tramplara, his natural insolence breaking through the varnish of politeness he had assumed. 'I refuse to be dictated to ; and I shall act as I choose with both missie's money and with that owl of a Squire.'

'One moment,' said Herring, whose cheek was flushed with anger. 'I ask one question of the Countess. Is it still your wish that the Battishills be saved from ruin ?'

'Certainly I wish it.'

'Allow me to ask further, supposing the means of relieving them were at your disposal, would you act in the way I have suggested ? That is, supposing you had money independent of Mr. Trampleasure, would you invest it in the West Wyke mortgages ?'

'I would do so.'

'You are quite sure of your own mind ?'

'I do not speak without meaning what I say.'

'Then, Mr. Trampleasure, you shall not lay a finger on the estate. It is safe. The money shall be forthcoming on the day you name to receive it.'

'Are you going to find it ?'

'That in no way concerns you.'

'If you are, you are softer than I supposed.'

'The money will be ready for you.'

Mirelle rose, and, stepping up to Herring,
held out her hand. There was more feeling in
her voice and warmth in her hand than before.

'I thank you, Mr. Herring. I am not
ungrateful.'

'What for ?' asked Tramplara, rudely.

'For crossing your plans,' she said, and
turned to look out of the window at the
view.

CHAPTER XVIII.

SALTING A MINE.

TRAMPLARA paid several visits to Upaver without calling at West Wyke, sometimes alone and sometimes along with his son. He did more than visit Upaver: he got some men to break ground there and begin a mine, without asking permission of the landlord, Mr. Battishill, or letting him know what he was about. The farmer who rented Upaver held his tongue.

One day, however, old Tramplara came to West Wyke House, along with a person whose looks betrayed what he was—a dissenting minister: in fact, the Reverend Israel Flamank.

Mr. Battishill was by no means pleased to receive Tramplara. A mouse is not elated at the sight of the cat.

Nothing, however, could be more friendly than the manner of Tramplara. He was

gushing and jovial. He presented his friend
Mr. Flamank, under whom, he said, to his
soul's welfare he had sat, one whom he should
always regard as, under Providence, the man
who had brought him to realise the great
value of eternity and the infinite nothingness
of to-day. Then followed a great deal of this
sort of unctuous flattery, 'laid on with a
trowel' and sticking wherever applied. Mr.
Battishill looked on with amused surprise to
see how readily Mr. Flamank accepted the
splashes, coarse and thick as they were.

Then Tramplara addressed himself directly
to the Squire.

'You must allow me, Battishill, to shake
your hand once more; you must indeed. My
friend and shepherd, Flamank, has made a
discovery—a discovery of such moment that
I doubt not it will astonish you. That it will
please you, I do not doubt either. Flamank
is a divine who has made prophecy his special
study, and his knowledge of Bible history and
geography is simply surprising. By the way,
before I tell you what his find is, will you
let me know whether you really propose to pay
me back in full what I advanced some years
ago?'

'I shall not be able to do so,' answered
Mr. Battishill, 'but a friend has offered to

find the money, and to relieve you of the mortgages.'

'You mean young Herring.'

Mr. Battishill nodded.

'But where the devil'—Mr. Flamank started and looked remonstratingly at Tramplara—'where in Deuteronomy—I said Deuteronomy,—he can have come upon the money, I can't think. I did know something about old Jago Herring, his father, and I thought he had been a plate licked pretty clean. I did not suppose there was much fat left sticking. But I dare say the old woman had money.'

'What old woman?'

'Mrs. Jago Herring, the lieutenant's mother. And as there was no daughter, her money naturally came to him. It is possible that is how he must have come by it. Where is he now?'

'In London, I believe. He left a week or two ago.'

'I may take it for granted, I suppose, that the money will be forthcoming?' asked Mr. Trampleasure.

'I do not doubt it. Mr. Herring is a man of his word,' answered the old Squire.

'I congratulate you, Battishill.' Mr. Battishill winced each time he was addressed

with familiarity. 'I congratulate you. It
would have gone hard with me to sell you up.
I would not have done it unless forced to do
so. What drove me to threaten was need of
money, and the occasion of needing it I leave
to my reverend friend here to unfold.
Whether I am wise in trusting him, I cannot
say. But what is a pastor for but to lead ?
But I must open the case, he is too modest to
tell the tale, as it redounds to his honour and
is a brilliant example of sagacity. I must tell
you, Battishill, that I have been privileged to
attend his Bible lectures, and he has deeply
impressed me with the greatness and com-
mercial enterprise of the Philistines.'

' Phœnicians, of course,' said Flamank.

' Phœnicians, of course—you see, Squire,
I'm not well up in the story. I follow my
guide, but all this lore is puzzling to me.
Well, you know the Phœnicians came to
Cornwall to fetch tin and gold, and that
Solomon's servants came along with the servants of Hiram for the purpose, and they
brought the tin and the gold to Jerusalem for
the temple.'

' Mr. Battishill must have heard of the
Phœnicians,' said Mr. Flamank, now on his
particular ground, and able to trot. ' From
them we derive clotted cream. It is a singular

and significant fact that clotted cream is made
nowhere in the world except in Devon, Cornwall, and Phœnicia. That is a well-esta-
blished fact, and it speaks volumes in favour
of an early intercourse between the Cassiterides and the natives of Tyre and Sidon.
The Cassiterides have been for some time
identified in the minds of antiquaries with
Devon and Cornwall. The only difficulty
in the way is this. The Cassiterides are described by the ancient geographers as islands.
But the difficulty vanishes when closely considered. The Phœnicians ascended Brown
Willy and Cosdon, and from these heights
saw the sea on both sides, and, not supposing
they were in an isthmus, they hastily and
incorrectly concluded they were in an island.
But the fact of clotted cream being found only
in Phœnicia and the West of England is, to
my mind, absolutely conclusive. A point not
considered by antiquaries has arrested my
attention. The point is, that the Jews came
with the Phœnicians, and that they actually
formed permanent settlements in our West
Country.'

'Jews, Jews!' put in Tramplara : 'they
would go after tin anywhere.'

'Look at Marazion,' continued Mr. Flamank ; 'the Bitter Waters of Zion. The place

bears the stamp of its origin in its name.
There is Port Isaac, also, no doubt named
after the patriarch, and Jacobstow, and,
touching memorial, Davidstow, so called after
the sweet psalmist by the servants of his son
Solomon. There is a hamlet of Herodsfoot,
and a village of Issey, that is, Isaiah, and St.
Sampson, after the strongest of men. Still
more remarkable is the fact of the Israelitish
colonists founding a parish which they called
Temple, because they were at the time engaged on building that wondrous structure in
Jerusalem. Redruth derives its name from
the ancestress of David, and we still speak of
sending persons to Jericho, which is a farm
not far distant from Launceston. A careful
study of the Scriptures led me some time
ago to this conclusion, that what the profane
writers call the Cassiterides are, in the sacred
page, called Ophir.'

'Ophir—"over the sea and far away!"
You recall the text, Squire,' interjected Tramplara.

'Our friend's familiarity with the Scriptures is late, and not as accurate as might be
desired,' apologised Mr. Flamank, with a look
of pity cast at Tramplara. 'Suffice it that,
led by a delicate chain of evidence as clear
and unmistakable as that of clotted cream, I

was led to seek Ophir in these western
counties. You will recall that the inspired
penman lays down the situation of Ophir with
great nicety. It lies between Mesha and
Sephar. * Now Mesha is undeniably Meshaw
in North Devon, and Sephar is Sheepstor in
South Devon. Draw a line between Meshaw
and Sheepstor, and it passes over Cosdon.'

'Why, bless my heart,' exclaimed Mr. Battishill, 'you are not going to find Ophir here!'

'We have found it,' said the dissenting
minister, gleefully. 'The identification is complete. Do you happen to see my "Western
Cornucophir"?'

'Cornucophir, what is that?'

'My paper—a monthly originally entitled
the Cornucopia, because of the abundance of
good things it contained. When this surprising discovery dawned on me, I changed
the name to Cornucophir—Cornu, for Cor-
nubia, Cornwall, and Ophir, for the Land of
Gold. The combination is happy.'

'But you are looking for Ophir in Devon,
not in Cornwall.'

'Devon was included in Cornwall till the
time of Athelstan, who drove the Britons
back over the Tamar, and restricted them to
Cornwall. Tamar'—Mr. Flamank paused
and rubbed his hands—'there again, the river

called after the daughter of David and twin
sister of Absalom. Having arrived at this
remarkable discovery by an exhaustive process and irrefragable evidence, in which every
step is capable of being demonstrated with
mathematical certainty to Christian believers,
I begged Mr. Trampleasure, who has wide
experience in mines——'

'Polpluggan,' groaned Mr. Battishill.

'As in Polpluggan, as you rightly observe,
to examine the line between Meshaw and that
mountain in the east, Sheepstor. Mr. Trampleasure is not as sanguine in this matter as I
am. He is hard to be convinced even now ;
I am not sure that his faith is firm. Whilst
we were discussing the nature of the land
between Meshaw and Sheepstor—he resolutely
refused to explore the red sandstone and clay
land, maintaining that gold is never found
except in the proximity of granite—he told me
of a farm of yours called Ophir.'

'Ophir!' exclaimed the old gentleman; 'I
have no such farm.'

'Excuse me,' said Mr. Flamank ; 'you
have, and I have been over it myself, exploring the ground for gold.'

'I believe you call the place Upaver,' said
Tramplara, with a twinkle in his eye, which
watched the Squire intently.

'Upaver! You have not been hunting up my silver lead mine, have you?'

'Silver lead, no!' answered the pastor; 'we have been hunting for gold.'

'But this is stark nonsense,' exclaimed Mr. Battishill; 'the place never was called Ophir. It is, and always has been, Upaver.'

'Upaver and Ophir are all the same, just as Sheepstor is the same as Sephar. I asked the farmer the name of the place, and without hesitation he said that he minded in old times it was called Ophir, but that the maps spell it with an *U.*'

'He has not been fifteen years on the farm, and I have been here seventy.'

'He has heard from the oldest inhabitant.'

'I am the oldest inhabitant,' protested Mr. Battishill. 'I can show you, moreover, leases of a hundred and two hundred years ago, in which it is called Upaver.'

'The leases were drawn up by lawyers ignorant of the pronunciation of the name. What the farmer told me was confirmed by another man, an old wild-looking creature, almost a savage. He also said the place was called Ophir, and he clenched his statement with a dreadful imprecation on all those who called it otherwise. What is more, he showed me a silver coin he had found, and I bought it of him for five shillings. If you will examine it, you will see Hebrew characters on it. I have seen this coin figured in Commentaries on the Bible ; on the obverse a vase, the pot of manna, I presume, on the reverse a flower, Aaron's blooming rod. It is a shekel. Now I ask you, how came a shekel to be found at Ophir unless the Israelites had been there to drop it ?'

Mr. Battishill took the coin, and turned it over in his hand. He was puzzled.

' That man you describe is old Grizzly Cobbledick, who lives under the Giant's Table.'

' I have seen the Giant's Table. It is an Israelitish monument, a Gilgal. There are many such in Cornwall, as well as upright stones—the same that Jacob set up and anointed with oil.'

' There are plenty of these upright stones on Dartmoor,' said Mr. Battishill. ' On the side of Belstone Tor is a circle called the Nine Maidens. The story goes that they were damsels so fond of dancing that they would not desist on the Sunday, and in consequence were turned to stone. And it is said that even now on Sunday at noon the stones come to life and dance thrice round in a circle.'

'I must make a note of this for my article in the "Western Cornucopbir." I pray you to observe the continuance of Sabbatical ideas, an evidence of Jewish teaching ; and of the resistance to it on Belston Tor, a mountain dedicated to Bel or Baal, the Sun God of the Phœnicians.'

'But you are holding back from Mr. Battishill the most important discovery of all,' said Tramplara, who saw that the old gentleman was not much impressed by the biblical and antiquarian theories of his visitor.

'At my request, and against his own convictions,' continued Mr. Flamank, 'my good friend Trampleasure searched Ophir for gold. A more qualified person could not have been found, for he is thoroughly conversant with the metals and their ores. He brought me one day some sand, granite washings, with grains in it that certainly looked like gold. We tested them with nitric acid, and, sure enough, they proved to be gold. I had no rest in my mind till I had persuaded Mr. Trampleasure to accompany me to Ophir, and to assist me in the examination of the place. He conducted me to the spot where he had found the gravel, and there we searched and I found this.'

He held out some shining yellow cubes.

'That is mundic,' said Mr. Battishill; 'it looks like gold, but is worthless.'

'So Mr. Trampleasure said. He laughed at me for my mundic find, but I could hardly be convinced that it was not gold. However, later, I found these grains. Here they are in my kerchief, with the quartz and mica as I took them up. I did not find much, but still, enough to show that the metal is present.'

He spread out his handkerchief on the table. In the midst of the coarse white gravel were certain yellow granules that looked like gold.

'You found this in Upaver valley?' asked Mr. Battishill, in great surprise.

'Yes, I was more successful than Trampleasure. But then I worked in faith, and he was dubious, so I dare say looked with less eagerness.'

'This is very extraordinary,' said the old gentleman. 'I never suspected the existence of gold on my property.'

'Why not?' asked Trampleasure. 'Gold is always found in connection with granite.'

'That is true; but none has been found hitherto in Devon.'

'And yet the whole valley has been streamed by miners in olden times. Their mounds of refuse are traceable all the way to the source of the stream. No gold has been sought because none was expected to be found. The Bible has led me, by a course of inductive evidence, to the identical spot whence came the gold that overlaid the temple, and that made the shields with which Solomon adorned the walls of his palace.'

'Whence that gold was got, more gold must be obtainable,' put in Tramplara; 'especially with our modern appliances.'

'It is most amazing,' said Mr. Battishill. 'Bless me! I wish I were well enough to get out; but I am stricken, and can only creep about with the aid of a stick. I should like myself to examine the place where you say you found the gold.'

'Surely you cannot doubt my word,' said Mr. Flamank. 'I can give you the best possible proof of my sincerity. I am ready to embark my little savings to the last penny in the mines of Ophir, if you will consent to their being worked.'

'I have no objection whatever, so long as I am not asked to risk any money in them myself.'

'Look you here, Squire,' said Tramplara; 'let us strike whilst the iron is hot. I am as anxious as the Reverend Flamank about

Ophir. You can lose nothing, and may make a pot of money. I have brought with me a lease ; read it. I will pay you a yearly rental of a hundred pounds, and you shall have the usual royalties on the gold raised. Then I will undertake to form a company to work the mines of Ophir. Not one penny can you lose by it. If you choose to take shares you may run some risk, not otherwise. If the mine proves a success, your fortune will be made, and so will mine, and those other lucky devils——'

'Lucky what ?' inquired the startled pastor.

'Lucky devotees, I said. I said devotees distinctly. Those lucky devotees who took shares in Ophir. " Out of the hills ye shall dig brass," said the great lawgiver, and his prophecy will be fulfilled, for brass in colloquial English means money.'

Tramplara took a lease out of his pocket and opened it before Mr. Battishill.

'Read it—nothing can be fairer.'

'Father,' said Cicely, who had come in, 'please do nothing till Mr. Herring returns. Take his advice before signing any document.'

'Nonsense, my dear ; I can lose nothing. I

shall not take a share, and I may gain thousands of pounds.'

'If you will work the mine yourself, do so,' said Tramplara: 'if not, let us work it. The religious public is already screwed up to a pitch of screaming excitement. The " Western Cornucopia "——'

' " Cornucophir," ' corrected the pastor. ' Besides, I object to the term screaming excitement.'

' It is allegorical and Oriental—Phœnician, in fact,' explained Tramplara. ' The " Cornu-cophir " has been leading them on week by week, expecting the discovery of Ophir. Now all is ready for the announcement that it has been found, and with that announce-ment we must publish the prospectus of the Ophir Gold Mining Company. If you do not accept my terms, all I can say is, the place will be invaded by religious gold-diggers, who will turn everything topsy-turvy and carry off every particle of gold they find without giving you any share in their spoil.'

' I will sign the lease; it is only for a year,' said Mr. Battishill, eagerly ; ' but I can take no shares, I have not the money.'

' I will take as many as I can,' said the minister. ' Ophir must succeed.'

' Now then ! ' shouted Tramplara, waving

the lease over his head. ' Now for the run of
gold. Blow the trumpet in Zion; call the
solemn assembly of sharetakers together. I
shall be ready for them with my crushing
machines. Hoorah for the gold of Ophir,
and the fortunes that will be made out of
it!'

CHAPTER XIX.

TWO STRINGS TO ONE BOW.

CAPTAIN TRECARREL had the good luck to find Mirelle alone in the garden house, engaged on her flowers. She had not been taught to do useful work. She cut out lace patterns in paper, and made imitation flowers. She could play and sing, but there was no piano in the garden house, and she spent most of her time there, so as to be away from the rooms frequented by Trampleasure senior and junior.

Captain Trecarrel was playing his cards very carefully. He did not intend to be off altogether with the old love till he was quite sure that it was to his pecuniary advantage to be on with the new. He was curious to know in what Mirelle's money had been invested. This was not easy for him to find out. He could not inquire of old Tramplara.

After turning the matter over in his head,

the Captain resolved on trying to ascertain what he desired to know through Mirelle herself, who was too simple to suspect his purpose.

He took a seat by her in the window. She smiled at him, and made room beside her.

'I have been thinking a great deal about you, Mirelle,' said he. He had slipped into calling her by her Christian name, and she did not resent it. 'And the more I think of you, the more I pity you. Your poor dear father made a sore mistake in confiding you to the care of these Trampleasures.'

'They were his relations,' she said.

'True; but then you are so utterly out of place among them. You are unable to sympathise with them——'

'Fortunately.'

'Fortunately, indeed, or you would not be charming. A grievous error has been committed, I may even say that a great wrong has been done you, unintentionally, and the consequence is that you suffer. I see it in your face.'

'Captain Trecarrel,' said Mirelle, 'I once thought to myself, suppose Heaven were to rob me of all means, and I were obliged to be a servant maid in the kitchen, then I thought

how utterly unable I should be to live in
such a place, not because it was a kitchen,
but because of those I should have to asso-
ciate with. I and they would have no interests, no pursuits, no ambitions, hardly a
thought in common. To all intents I might
as well live in a stable with horses, or in a
fowlhouse surrounded by cackling pullets. I
should not mind in the least shelling peas,
for I could think my own thoughts whilst so
engaged ; but to be encompassed with others
who think no thoughts, who have no ideas
worth uttering, who live as to their outsides,
and have no inner life, that would be unendurable. I find myself now in such a situation. The Trampleasures and I do not see
the same sights nor hear the same sounds.
We have not even the sense of smell in common, for Mr. Tramplara and young Sampson
like to sniff brandy and puff bad tobacco, and
I am convinced that Orange and her mother
do not dislike these, to me, intolerable odours.
In the garden is a sweet rose and a bed of
mignonette. I have not once seen a Trampleasure apply his nose to a flower. We
have the same organic structure, and are
classed together in natural history as belonging to the same genus, but there the simi-
larity ends. The likeness is superficial, the

dissimilarity is radical. The likeness is physical, the dissimilarity psychical. The Trampleasures are animals made in the likeness of man. I am human, made in the likeness of God. I can see what is beautiful in nature and art. I can feel music in my soul, I have aspirations beyond making money and getting married. I have interests beyond the claque of Launceston gossip. But these Trampleasures have no sense of beauty, no poetical instinct, no spiritual aspirations. Orange is the best of them, but in her I only think I perceive a soul, I am not sure that it exists. God took some of the beasts he had made and bade them stand up on their hind legs, that they might look at heaven instead of contemplating earth. But their souls did not stand up also. The result was the ape. There are men, likewise, not superior. They walk on two feet, but their souls run on all fours.'

'Poor Mirelle!' said Trecarrel, looking tenderly at her out of the Trecarrel blue eyes. 'Yours is a cruel fate.'

'Yes, it is cruel, and, but for this summerhouse where I can be alone, would be insupportable. Life to these Trampleasures, and people cast in their mould, is a harpsichord on which they drone a strain void of invention, freshness, and thought. When you have heard their performance—it is the song of life —you are aware that you have listened to a succession of notes unworthy of being termed a melody, in chords undeserving of being designated harmony. When one with higher thoughts sits down to the same instrument and plays a piece like a sonata of Beethoven, they yawn and say, " Let us have something out of the Beggars' Opera ! " '

Little did Mirelle guess how mean and commonplace was the barrel-organ tune that Captain Trecarrel cared to play on his harpsichord of life. Because he was a gentleman by birth, and a Catholic in faith, she supposed that he stood, like Saul, a head and shoulders higher than the vulgar beings that surrounded him and her. We shall see, in the sequel, how egregiously Mirelle was mistaken.

' Is there no escape for you ? ' asked the Captain.

' I see none. I should like to return to Paris, to the convent where I was reared, but Mr. Trampleasure will not hear of it. I should be quite content to be a nun.'

' A nun ! ' exclaimed Trecarrel. ' Oh no, no ! dear Mirelle, that must not be. With your gifts of mind and soul and person, you are suited to live and shine in the world.'

' In what world ? This mean, dull English world ?'

' Your place is here. Your heart has not
yet spoken. You are still young. Some day
you will make a good man happy, and you
will find your proper sphere of usefulness,
with a congenial spirit at your side, not in
shelling peas, but in spreading enlightenment among the dark and erring souls around
you.' His voice shook. He took her hand,
and he felt it tremble in his.

' No, Mirelle, you were not born to wither
in a convent unloved and unloving. Excuse
me if I give you my opinion with great plain-
ness. You are here without a guide. These
Tramplaras cannot advise you, because they
cannot understand your position. Trust me
as a brother. Let us regard each other in
the affectionate and familiar light of brother
and sister—that is our relationship in the
faith. Allow me to counsel you. My heart
aches when I think of your loneliness. I
place myself at your disposal: trust me, and
suffer me to be your adviser.' He raised her
hand to his lips, and kissed it fervently.
The little hand shrank back, and when he
looked up he saw alarm in her dark eyes.

' A brotherly kiss,' he said, reassuringly,

'the seal of our bond, nothing more.   Shall it
be so ?'

'The seal will not need renewal,' she answered.

He saw that her eyes were filling.   He
knew that she liked him ; he was doing his
best to make her love him.   It would be easy
for him to advance from brotherly to lover-
like affection, and it was quite possible to
remain stationary on fraternal regard.   This
he thought to himself, and he said in his own
soul, 'Bravo, Trecarrel ! you have not compromised yourself by a word.'

'And now, dear sister Mirelle,' he said,
with his sweetest smile, 'the thing I desire to
know is, What has become of your father's
money ?'

She was surprised.   He saw it ; but he
went on quietly, 'You see in what a brotherly
and practical spirit I approach your affairs.
I want to know exactly how you stand, for—
between four eyes be it spoken—I am not
satisfied that a certain whitehaired person
who shall be nameless is the most prudent
man to be intrusted with money.   He sank a
large sum in Patagonians which might just
as well have been sunk in Cranmere pool.
If he made a fool of himself with his own
money, he may play the fool also with

yours. For how long is he your trustee?'

'For five years. I am eighteen, and I do
not come of age till I am twenty-three.'

'Unless you marry.' Trecarrel sighed,
and looked hard at the distant peaks of Dartmoor.

'I do not think there is anything about
my marriage in the will, which I have read,
and I know the contents.'

'Oh!' said the Captain, and his mouth
went down at the corners. 'You do not come
into possession at marriage.'

'I believe not—not till I am three-and-
twenty.'

The Captain released the tips of Mirelle's
fingers which he had seized when he put the
question.

'Then Tramplara has the entire and uncontrolled disposal of the money for five years,
and if you were to marry now you would
still have to wait five years till you got it—
if you got it, in the end, at all.'

'I suppose so.'

'Do you happen to know what the old
fellow has invested your money in? I ask
as a friend, because I wish to protect your
interests, and to advise you what you should
do.'

' I have already had an adviser here—Mr. Herring: he was anxious about the money.'

' He was, was he ?' Captain Trecarrel drew nearer, with revived interest, and again attempted to possess himself of the hand, but failed.

' Yes, he appeared very anxious.'

' On what grounds? What possible right had he to inquire about it?'

' He expressed friendly regard for me.'

' A sort of brotherly interest?' inquired the Captain.

' No,' answered Mirelle, curtly, and drew herself up. The Captain looked hard at her.

' Have you given him any encouragement? Have you allowed him any right to interfere?'

Mirelle's cheek coloured, and a haughty flash came into her eye.

' Captain Trecarrel, I do not comprehend you.'

' My dear Mirelle,' he said in a gentle, soothing tone, ' do not misunderstand me. What I mean is harmless enough not to offend you. Did you ask his advice, and in your first loneliness give him such occasion as to suppose that he was necessary, that as a pert and pushing cock-sparrow he has hopped in where not wanted, since you have come under the protection of others?'

'No,' answered Mirelle, 'I have always kept him at a distance. When he has volun-. teered help it has been declined. He came here about the money not for my sake only, but for the sake of some friends whom he wanted to assist out of a difficulty.'

'Oh! he wanted to help friends to your money! How disinterested and how bene-volent!'

'He wished to have my money invested in mortgages on the estate of West Wyke.'

'What did Mr. Trampleasure say to that?'

'He absolutely refused. He said he had a better investment in view, one that would render double.'

'What was that?—not Patagonia?'

'No; Ophir.'

'What! The gold mines of Ophir?'

'Yes, my money is to be put into that.'

Captain Trecarrel vented a low whistle, and stood up quickly. 'Dear Countess, always command my services—as a friend,' he said. 'Excuse my flight, I must have a word with Tramplara at once.'

He hurried from the summer-house, and entered the front door of Dolbeare. He was so often there that he no longer went through

the formality of ringing. It was Liberty Hall, .
as Tramplara assured all his friends.

He tapped at the dining-room door and
went in.

There he found Mr. Tramplara smoking
and working at accounts. Orange sat near
the window ; she had been speaking with her
father, and had been crying. Both father and
daughter rose hastily as the Captain came in,
and Trecarrel had sufficient penetration to see
that he had been their topic.

'Halloo, Captain!' exclaimed the old man,
turning almost purple. 'Talk of the—hum,
and he is sure to appear, as the psalmist says.
The very man I wanted to see. How are
you?'

Orange slipped out of the room.

'Sit down, Captain, and let us have a
talk. Fact is, I want particularly to have a
bone picked with you. There is Orange, poor
girl, wasting to a shadow. You are not dealing fairly by her ; you are engaged, and yet
you won't come to the scratch. She says you
are tateytating with the other party on the
trotters, as Mirelle calls the pavement, and
give Orange the gutter to walk in. That
won't do.'

'You entirely mistake me,' said Trecarrel,
his blue eye becoming cold ; he drew himself

up, and began to point his moustache, whilst he looked Trampleasure over contemptuously. 'Do you dare to insinuate that I—a gentleman, a Trecarrel—am behaving otherwise than honourably ? I love your daughter as much as I loved her at first ; but you and I are men of the world, and we both know that love and onions are poor commodities on which to keep house. You are well aware what my circumstances are, for I have concealed nothing from you ; and you must therefore know that I cannot, as a gentleman and a man of honour, invite a lady to share my future with me unless she be prepared to provide pepper and salt with which to season the onions.'

'I know that. Orange is not penniless.'

'No, but Patagonian bonds are not nourishing, Mr. Trampleasure.'

'Who said that Orange would bring nothing else with her?'

'You offered me five thousand pounds with her in securities which are worthless.'

'I offered you those bonds before I knew they would depreciate so greatly. They may recover any day.'

'I incline to wait for that day before setting up house with Miss Orange.'

'Nonsense, Trecarrel. If you won't take these bonds, you shall have some sounder

stuff. I am a man of my word. I said I
would give Orange five thousand pounds, and
five thousand she shall have, the day she is
married.'

' In bonds?'

'In shares, if you like, in one of the most
promising of all ventures.'

' In Ophir—no, thank you.'

' You are a fool to refuse them. Why,
man! have you read the " Cornucopia "? Have
you seen the prospectus of the company?'

' Mr. Trampleasure, I will have no paper
at all. Give me with Orange the sum of five
thousand down, and insure me five thousand
more when you are dead, and I will ask her
to name the day.'

' You are mercenary.'

' I am practical. You know that Trecarrel will support a bachelor—that is, keep
him in mutton chops and fried potatoes, and
a new coat twice a year. I will give you a
sample of my penury. Whenever I have
apple-tart for dinner, I think twice before I
indulge myself with clotted cream over it.
My circumstances will not allow me to support a wife and family. I am bound to look
ahead, and to consider my wife's interest as
well as my own. I cannot offer her the
humiliations of poverty.'

'Well, well,' said Tramplara, 'you shall have the money down.'

'Your word?'

Tramplara held out his hand, 'I give it you.'

'I should prefer it in black and white,' said the Captain.

'You shall have it in yellow and white,' said the old man. 'And now in return you shall grant me a favour—your name as a director of the Ophir Gold Mining Company.'

'My name is Trecarrel,' answered the Captain, freezingly.

'I know that well enough—that is why I want it.'

'And that is precisely why you shall not have it.'

'You refuse me this favour?'

'Emphatically. I do not believe in Ophir.'

The old man drummed with his fingers on the table, and raised his eyes furtively to the Captain, met his cold, supercilious stare, and dropped them again.

'Well! go into the drawing-room, and patch up the rent with Orange.'

Then, when the Captain was gone, Tramplara laughed heartily. 'By Grogs!' he said, 'who would have thought the fellow so keen? He don't look it.'

The Captain found Orange standing in the drawing-room leaning against the mantelpiece, tearing a white lily that she had plucked out of a vase into many pieces. Her fingers were stained with the pollen. Her cheeks were flushed, and an angry glitter was in her eyes, twinkling through tears of mortified pride.

Trecarrel had not much difficulty in changing the expression of that handsome face, and before he left the reconciliation was complete, sealed with a kiss, and the day was named.

CHAPTER XX.

GRINDING GOLD.

In a remarkably short space of time two 'leats,' that is, channels of water, had been brought from Rayborough Pool along the side of the moor to the site of the gold mine. Buildings had been erected, wooden sheds run up and tarred, and a crushing machine was in operation. One stream of water was conducted over a wheel, and the wheel set in motion half a dozen hammers that pounded the granite ; then the granite thus pounded was passed under an iron roller which effectually reduced it to powder. This powder was made to slide through a trough into water brought by the second leat, and the water, as soon as it received the pounded quartz, became milky. The milky water overflowed into a second tank, depositing in both much that was held in solution, and then ran away into the river, which it discoloured for some distance down.

Old Tramplara looked regretfully at the white water. If Ophir had been nearer Plymouth or Exeter, he might have sold it as milk.

The deposit in the tanks was subjected to a second and, indeed, a third washing. It was washed and rewashed till all the quartz had been carried away and nothing remained but glittering gold.

The excitement created by the discovery of Ophir was prodigious. The neighbourhood came to see the works. The miners extracted granite, and placed the pieces under the stampers, and then transferred the gravel into which they had been pounded to the roller. Any one might watch the process. Everything was above board; there was no attempt at concealment. Only, no one was allowed to approach the precious deposit unattended by the overseer. Any respectable person was allowed to follow the washing and drying to the final process, where nothing remained but the costly yellow grains. All he had to do was to write for permission to Mr. Tramplara, or to send in his card at the works, and leave to go over the entire mine—without any reserve—was freely accorded. The number of crowns and guineas pocketed by the very respectable overlooker

ripened the fruits of civilisation in him. He
became courteous, eager to instruct, pious, and
sober. Christian graces grew on golden roots.
There was a fixed time in the day when
visitors were given admission to the mine.

The limitation of time was rendered necessary by reason of the crowd of visitors eager
to examine the works, and the consequent
interference with the working. The regula-
tion was reasonable and unassailable. Another
rule was made that no one was to be allowed
to go within arm's length of, nor to handle
the gold after final washing. The overseer,
however, made exceptions in favour of every
respectable visitor, letting him understand
that the exception in his case was unique, and
only granted because of his—the visitor's—
really extraordinary respectability. He was
allowed to gather up in his palm and turn
over with his finger the golden dust, and the
polite and pious overlooker always reaped
a rich harvest from this exceptional favour.

Readers of the 'Western Cornucophir'
came from all parts of Cornwall; serious men,
with heavy brows, big jaws, and firm lipless
mouths. Women also—married women, likewise serious, (unmarried women, speaking
broadly, are flighty,) in rich but sober dresses,
arrived in chaises, wearing spectacles and

false fronts, and having bibles in their pockets, and vinegary attendants carrying shawls, and guardians of their virtue. There were many Methodical Christian, and Unmethodical Christian, and Primitive Christian, and Latter Day Christian, and Universal Christian, and Particular Christian, and Ne-plus-ultra Christian ministers, all intensely interested in Ophir, taking up the matter as one of *stantis vel cadentis ecclesiæ.* These were treated with exceptional courtesy at the mine, by express command of Mr. Tramplara. They were shown everything. They were set to work themselves in the adit. They galled their soft palms in picking at the gold vein, or granite supposed to contain the vein of gold. They carried the lumps of their own extraction to the crusher. They watched them being pounded and rolled, not turning an eye away the whole time. They assisted at the washing. They picked out the gold themselves from the pan, and were liberally allowed to carry home with them each at least a guinea's worth of the precious grains. Thereupon each became in his special circle an agent of the company. And Methodical Christian, and Unmethodical Christian, and Primitive Christian, and Latter Day Christian, and Universal Christian, and Particular Christian, and Ne-plus-ultra Christian applications for shares, poured in by every post.

But the greatest hit of all was the solemn opening and dedication of Ophir.

A huge tent had been hired from Exeter, capable of seating many hundred persons. Bunting in profusion, of every colour, fluttered from it. Over the entrance rose a flagstaff from which waved a gold-coloured banner adorned with the Seal of Solomon.

A cannon had been brought from Exeter, and it was discharged at intervals. The Okehampton band was engaged, and it played out of tune alternately with a military band from Exeter, which played in tune, and rivalled it in the worthlessness of the music performed.

The day was magnificent. An autumn day, with a glorious sun illumining the moorland rosy with blooming heather, as though raspberry cream had been spilt over the hillsides. The scarlet uniforms of the band, the gay colours of the flags, the white tent, the glitter of the falling water over the wheel, combined to form a charming scene. All Okehampton, all North and South Tawton and Chagford was there, and many also from Tavistock, Launceston, Moreton Hampstead, and Exeter. The people were scattered over

the moor slopes, listening to the music which
was not worth listening to, in the way in
which English people do listen—that is, talking the whole time ; they raced and rolled
over on the short grass, and strewed the hillsides with sandwich papers and empty ginger-
beer bottles. Ginger-beer bottles ! ay, and
bottles of cold tea. For Ophir was a great
Temperance mine, and the dedication of Ophir
a Temperance demonstration, Ri-lid-de-riddle-
roll! Who cannot rollick on ginger-beer?
Who that is by nature inane can fail to make
an ass of himself when out on a holiday on
cold tea?

Ophir was a great Temperance mine. All
the washers were sworn in as total abstainers.
As was stated on the prospectus, the workings were to be carried on only with water.
'We may as well fish in two ponds, Sampy,'
said old Tramplara ; 'let us angle for the
Temperites as well as for the Israelites.'

Thus the dedication of Ophir was not
only a grand religious demonstration for all
those who looked for Israel in England, but
also of those who have supplanted the Ten
Commandments by one, 'Thou shalt not
drink fermented liquor.' Old Tramplara was
desirous to have the mines blessed by ministers of all denominations—twelve, if possible,

to represent the twelve tribes. He had therefore applied to the bishop of the diocese, and
requested his presence for the opening of the
proceedings. But the bishops of the Angli-
can Church are not the tugs that lead, but
the boats that follow, popular opinion. They
bless nothing till authorised to do so by the
daily papers, and as the daily papers had not
yet spoken on the subject of Ophir, the bishop
was in the bewildered condition of the priest
of Delphi when the oracle is silent. If Ophir
were to prove a magnificent success, he would
never forgive himself for not having been
at the opening. If it proved a disastrous
failure, he would never forgive himself for not
staying away. So he temporised, after the
manner of weak men and weak classes of men ;
he discovered that he was due at the opening
of a (barrel) organ at the Land's End on that
particular day, and he wrote a letter full of
apologies, expressive of his warmest interest
in the proceedings, promising his heartfelt
prayers, invoking the most solemn blessings
on the gathering, and then ate his breakfast,
devoured the ' Times,' and forgot everything
about Ophir and the barrel organ at the
Land's End.

But though the bishop of the diocese was
unavoidably absent, representative pastors of

all the Christian denominations in the West
were present, and prayed and harangued to
their hearts' content, and ate and drank to
their stomachs' content as well.

The tent was filled to overflowing. Grace
was said simultaneously by twenty-nine ministers to avoid giving offence by exalting one
above another. A noble collation had been
provided. Waiters dressed like clergymen
attended on the guests. 'Lemonade, sir?'
'Gooseberriade, ma'am?' as they uncorked
long-necked bottles with gold foil about the
throats, and poured the effervescing drink
into champagne glasses. 'Temperance cake,
miss?' with an offer of an inviting dish of
sponge-cake sopped in—well, non-alcoholic
brandy—and with flummery over it to hide
its blushes.

Reporters were present from every West
of England paper and several London journals
as well. These gentlemen were supplied freely
with ' gooseberriade,' and grew cheery in spirit,
and red in face, and watery in eye, and un-
critical in disposition under its influence. They
began to believe in Ophir as much as a re-
porter can believe in anything. And when,
on raising the napkins under their finger-
glasses, each found a ten-pound note, the
enthusiasm of the press for Ophir bordered on

fanaticism. After lunch, the entire party
sought the mine, and those who could get in
hammered at the stone, and there was much
ado in wheeling to the stampers the 'gozzen'
that had been extracted.

Tramplara particularly urged on the reporters to dig and wash for themselves, and
they complied with his request. The prayers
and blessings of the pastors of discordant
Christianity had been of avail. Never before
had the rock yielded so much gold. There it
was — in glittering granules — strewing the
washing floor. The rock had been quarried
by ten reporters, seven pastors, and one old
lady, with a grim face and severely plain,
untrimmed costume. The stone had been
wheeled by them to the crushers, at that time
clear of every particle of stone. The grim old
lady had not wheeled, but carried her specimens in her gown, exposing thereby some
elaborate lace frills beneath it. The entire
party saw the granite thus extracted washed
in several waters. They washed it themselves,
no workman touched any part of the ma-
chinery, or dipped a finger into the water, and
there — there was the gold — gold-dust in
abundance. There could be no deception.
There was no room for deception.

John Herring was there also, looking on,

much puzzled. He had not been at the lunch, but had strolled to Ophir after it. His lead mine was not advanced. No company was formed to work it. Who would look at lead when gold was available? He watched the whole process critically, and was convinced that there was no deception in what passed under his eye. There the gold was. Every one present was given a grain as a memorial of that day. The whole affair was marvellous. The expense to which Tramplara had gone was prodigious. Would he have thrown his gold away in shovelfuls unless he were sure of getting gold out of the mine? Herring was young and simple. He was right. Tramplara would not have gone to this lavish expense unless he had made sure of getting gold out of the mine? But then, it did not follow that he was going to extract it from the granite. Some things are softer than granite, and the gold may be got easily enough by those who can touch the vein.

'What! Lieutenant! you here?' exclaimed Mr. Trampleasure, coming up to Herring, looking flushed and glossy. 'Glorious day, this. Wonderful discovery, this Ophir. "Thither the tribes go up!" said the prophet, speaking of this day and the way in which they went into the tent to their dinner. Come

in and have a glass of wi—, of something
comforting but not exhilarating. Come in, my
dear lieutenant; there is only the band there,
making clean the cup and the platter, when
their betters have done.'

'No, thank you,' answered Herring, 'I
have had an early dinner. Besides, I must
trouble you no longer to style me lieutenant.'

'Why so?'

'Because I have sold out.'

'Sold out! Become a civilian again!'

'Yes. I have things to attend to which
demand my presence here. I am going to
work the silver lead.'

'My dear fellow, don't throw money away
on that. Take shares in gold.'

'I prefer lead.'

'Herring, is that why you are taking up
the mortgages on West Wyke?'

'Partly.'

'You'll never work the lead yourself?
You have no experience. However, we will
talk of that another time. Are you likely to
be in Launceston next week?'

'Yes. I shall go there to pay you the
mortgage money.'

'Very well. We are going to have a kick
about on Thursday—the first dance in the

season. There is a reason : Orange is engaged
to Captain Trecarrel.   Will you come?'

Herring thought a while before answer-
ing.

' Look here ! I will tell that little bleached
puss of a missie to expect you, and put your
name down as her partner for the first caper.'

' I will come.'

All at once the Reverend Israel Flamank
was seen flying down the valley, with coat tails
expanded like wings, and his white tie loose
and flapping.   He was shouting and waving
his arms.

What was it?   Had he been bitten by a
serpent?   Had he found a nugget?

When he came up, he was breathless and
of inflamed countenance.   At length he
gasped—' I have been privileged to discover
it?'   Then he paused again.   A circle formed
round him.

' A do-deka-penta-hedron,' he said.   Then
seeing the reporters with their notebooks in
hand and pencils pausing in mid-air, and
fearing that their knowledge of Greek sur-
passed his (he need have entertained no apprehension), he added simply, ' Solomon's Seal
carved on a rock.'

The whole crowd went after him.   Here
was a wonderful coincidence !   Coincidence !

Avast! Conclusive evidence that the servants of Solomon had worked at this identical place. The symbol of Solomon, the interlacing triangles, cut in imperishable granite, was there as an eternal witness to Ophir.

Herring did not follow the troop : he turned to go back to West Wyke. He was not eager to inspect the ' Dodekapentahedron.'

END OF THE FIRST VOLUME.

LONDON : PRINTED BY
SPOTTISWOODE AND CO., NEW-STREET SQUARE
AND PARLIAMENT STREET

www.ingramcontent.com/pod-product-compliance
Lightning Source LLC
Chambersburg PA
CBHW021038030726
47496CB00006B/1600